FIGHT SONG

a novel

 JOSHUA MOHR ▪

Soft Skull Press
An Imprint of COUNTERPOINT
Berkeley

Fight Song © 2013 by Joshua Mohr

Library of Congress Cataloging-in-Publication Data
Mohr, Joshua.
Fight Song / Joshua Mohr.
pages cm
ISBN 978-1-59376-508-8 (pbk.)
1. Conduct of life—Fiction. 2. Self-realization—Fiction. I. Title.
PS3610.O669F54 2013
813'.6—dc23
2012040730

ISBN: 978-1-59376-508-8

Interior Design & Composition by Neuwirth & Associates
Cover Design by Michael Kellner

Printed in the United States of America

Soft Skull Press
An Imprint of COUNTERPOINT
1919 Fifth Street
Berkeley, CA 94710
www.softskull.com

Distributed by Publishers Group West

10 9 8 7 6 5 4 3 2 1

"*If you're afraid of the dark, remember the night rainbow.*
If there is no happy ending, make one out of cookie dough."

—COOPER EDENS

▪ The plock of despair ▪

Way out in a puzzling universe known as the suburbs, Bob Coffen rides his bike to work. He pedals and pants and perspires past all the strip malls, ripe with knockoff shoe stores, chain restaurants, emporiums stuffed with the latest gadgets, and watering holes deep enough that the locals can drown their sorrows in booze. Each plaza also contains at least one church, temple, or synagogue—a different way altogether to drown one's sorrows.

After arriving at the office, Coffen hightails it to the bathroom and wildly paper-towels away the pond of sweat from his crack. He works an unfortunate bundle in the back of his unzipped pants with such fury that the flab above Bob's belt shimmies in a kind of unintentional hula. He splashes water on his face, fixes his tie. He is overdressed and overheated and ready to slog through the stupor of another day at Dumper Games.

Bob plops down at his desk for only a few minutes before the head honcho of the company, Mister Malcolm Dumper himself, walks up, holding something behind his back. Dumper is only thirty, almost ten full years younger than Bob. He comes from family money (his grandfather was a Canadian oil tycoon). To show his north-of-the-border allegiances, Dumper always wears a throwback hockey sweater to work, Wayne Gretzky's #99 Edmonton Oilers jersey. To make matters worse, Dumper refers to himself as "the Great One," which was Gretzky's nickname on the ice.

But the most striking thing about Dumper is his tongue, thick and long, almost the size of a hot water bottle—when he focuses on ideas, crunching around their strengths and weaknesses, the floppy thing sort of lolls out front of his mouth.

"Do you know what today is?" Dumper asks Bob.

Coffen genuinely has no idea. "What is today?"

"The Great One would not forget such a momentous milestone," Dumper says. "Today is a fine wine. Today is an aged Bordeaux from the Left Bank."

"What's the occasion?" Bob says.

"It's your anniversary." Dumper pulls a wrapped present from behind his back and extends it to Coffen. "I would never forget what today means to this company because I would never forget what you mean to our little shop here, Bob. Congratulations on a decade of good times and good games, and our future together is as bright as a miner's helmet."

Bob takes the rectangular gift from him, surprised by how heavy it is. Surprised by the venomous burn going on in his heart—*I've been here for ten years?*

"Go on and open it, amigo," says Dumper. Coffen tears through the wrapping paper and stares at it for a few seconds. It's some sort of bulky wooden clock. He has no idea what to say and goes with, "Wow, I'm so honored by this unique timepiece."

"It's a plock. Half-plaque, half-clock. I named it myself."

On the face of the plock is engraved DEAR ROBERT COFFEN: IT'S ALWAYS TIME TO WORK!

The clock hands are not moving, fixed at midnight.

Bob frowns at the plock, and Dumper must notice his sourpuss face because he asks, "Don't you like it?"

"My name's not Robert."

"Bob is short for Robert. Everybody knows that."

"Sometimes, yes," Coffen says, "but I'm only Bob. On my birth certificate, it reads 'Bob Coffen.'"

At this, Dumper's frown gets even bigger than Bob's, the boss's humungous tongue creeping out and hanging there. After about ten seconds, he reels the lanky muscle back in and says, "Nobody's name is just Bob."

Coffen shrugs and says, "Bob is me."

"But besides this miniscule blip, the gist of the company's heartfelt sentiments remains the same. Robert . . . Bob . . . we at DG value all your effort to build games."

Bob wonders if a plock is the equivalent of giving a condemned man a final cigarette before the firing squad. He doesn't want to ponder all the wasted time, tries to distract himself with a task, turning the tragic contraption over in his hands, looking for a battery hatch or a way to plug it in to a power source. "How does the clock half work?"

"It doesn't," Dumper says.

"It's broken?"

"It's purely decorative."

Bob wants so much to tell his boss that he quits, but it comes out like this: "Thanks."

"We'll get your name right on the next one."

"Something to look forward to," says Coffen, speaking at a whisper.

Dumper shakes his head and storms off, muttering, "Nobody's only named Bob."

Alone, Coffen spends the rest of the day sitting right

like that, not doing one lick of work. He holds the heavy plock and watches how its hands never move. Always midnight. No way to document any of the expiring minutes, but damn if they aren't all disappearing.

▪ A despicable truth about
the human animal ▪

Bob's bike ride home that evening starts off much like the morning one. He is sweaty. Annoyed. He pedals past a billboard advertising Björn the Bereft, a magician/marriage counselor performing a few shows in town on his national tour. Coffen scowls at the billboard, knowing he and Jane will be catching the act this coming Friday. Actually, it didn't sound like the kind of thing that Jane would want to do in the first place, but she had been so insistent, Coffen went along with it—of course he went along with it! Isn't his fat ass oozed all over a bicycle seat because Jane wanted him to ride it, whip himself back into shape?

Coffen's not on the bicycle by himself: There's a corporate rucksack slung across his chest diagonally, the bandoleer of the working stiff. It pushes twenty pounds tonight because of the weighty plock.

He pedals and pants and perspires, turning onto a quiet stretch of residential road, riding in the bike lane, next to tall oleanders that line this street. His subdivision, his house, his wife, his kids, his computer and online life are only another half mile ahead.

Here's where Coffen's archenemy, Nicholas Schumann, pulls up next to Bob and his bike. Schumann slows his SUV, revs the engine, rolling down the passenger window so he can scream out at Coffen, "Shall we engage in a friendly test of masculine fortitude?"

Schumann is a douche of such a pungently competitive variety that he carries a picture of himself wearing his college football uniform in his wallet. And shows it to people. Bob will be huddled with the other dads of the subdivision at one barbecue or another and Schumann will whip out the photo and talk about how he single-handedly guided Purdue to an overtime win against the Fighting Irish of Notre Dame and how nobody thought they had a chance, but as the quarterback he had to keep his team focused, poised, grinding, etc., etc. All the neighborhood fathers hang on Schumann's probably fabricated remixes from his glory days. He has these dads trained to sniff out Bob's lack of interest in sports and has even said things in front of them like "Gentlemen, it appears that Coffen doesn't enjoy the great American pastime of pigskin."

They shake their astonished heads. Their eyes eyeing Bob like he pissed in the damn sangria.

"You really don't like the pastime of pigskin?" the disgusted dads ask.

"Football's fine," says Bob.

"Football is like storming the beaches of Normandy," Schumann says, the dads all nodding along. "It is a bunch of samurai let loose on the field to kill or be killed."

"I give up," Coffen mutters.

"That's your problem," says Schumann. "You can't give up. Not when Notre Dame's linebackers are blitzing your back side. Believe me, that's a life lesson."

Now, Coffen answers Schumann's request for a duel of masculine fortitude by saying, "You wanna race me?"

"Psycho Schumann wants to rumble."

"You have an unfair advantage."

"You'll have to be more specific," Schumann says. "I have about thirty advantages over you."

The plock's weight makes the bandoleer creep into Coffen's skin. "I mean the SUV is your advantage."

"I won't go over seven miles an hour. Come on: Let's see what you're made of."

It's a despicable truth about the human animal that people often thrust themselves into the crosshairs of unwinnable equations. Logic is meaningless. Lessons learned get heaved from windows. All that life experience jets the coop with myopic majesty, and it's here ye, here ye, gather round and take a gander as another dumb man makes a monkey out of himself.

Coffen's particular monkey-ness on this particular evening lies with the plock and the self-hate at being honored for wasting ten years of his life on a job that does nothing productive or interesting, a job that shines the light on the fact that Bob himself has settled into curdling routine. Rationally, he knows he can't beat Schumann—not piloting a bike while Schumann has a combustible engine—but Bob doesn't care. He can't care. There have been too many unwinnable contests in his life, and at this moment Coffen is hell-bent on seeing how he does against the Notre Dame pass rush, how he stacks up to what might be categorized as an insurmountable obstacle. Is he the kind of underdog that flouts expectations, or is Bob Coffen as miraculously pitiful as the subdivision fathers say?

So there Coffen is shirking the boring tradition of reason. There he is yelling to Schumann, "You're on, you rat bastard!"

And thus, the contest is underway.

So far, so good—Schumann stays at seven miles an hour. Coffen pulls ahead. He's winning! He's a full SUV-length ahead, and his lead is growing; all the sweating and panting and pain from the clawing bandoleer jabbing into Coffen are worth it. Adversity is a stepping-stone. It's in contests such as these that people disclose the true fight in their hearts, and Bob wants so badly to have fight left in his, despite the last decade's evidence to the contrary.

Next, Schumann has the vehicular gall to shatter the established ceiling of seven miles per hour. He pulls up even to Bob, flashes a Nicky All-American grin. Then he pulls ahead. Schumann toots the damn horn, toying with Coffen, slowing down and saying, "Ladies and gentlemen, they're neck and neck going into the homestretch . . ."

"You're speeding up," Bob says.

"Are you questioning my honor?"

"What's the speedometer say?"

"I fight fair and square," says Schumann, shaking his head, looking sinister. "Until I don't."

Here's when a certain self-celebrated college football hero reveals the existential interior of a rancorous cheater, edging his SUV a bit into the bike lane, almost clipping Coffen. Bob swerves into the rough patch of dead grass along the side of the road. Only a few feet before he'd be rammed into those unruly oleanders.

"Watch it," Bob says.

"Do you know what your problem is, Coffen?"

Still edging the SUV . . .

"I'm being run into an oleander?"

"You don't have any balls," Schumann says.

Bob will not be testicularly ridiculed. Hell no, he won't. Last week, last month, for the last ten years, yes, ridicule away, mock Bob like it's nobody's business. But tonight he's turning things around. Tonight, he hemorrhages pragmatism. Tonight, he cremates common sense, sends its ashes up into the atmosphere in a stunning cloud. What have these things brought him besides boredom, mediocrity?

"Fuck yourself, Schumann!" Bob says, taking his left hand off of the handle bar in preparation of giving Schumann the bird, except once his hand moves, the plock's weight makes the bike go herky-jerky, balance faltering, front wheel turning quickly to an unanticipated angle and Coffen flies over the handlebars.

He is airborne. He has left the bike behind and travels a few feet ahead of it, though this trip will be short-lived and soon his voyage shall transition into an excruciating landing.

The bike crashes, and so does Coffen.

The valiant Schumann doesn't even pump the brakes. He keeps driving. It's funny how people expose their camouflaged spirits in moments of emergency. Bob watches the taillights disappear.

▪ Hail Purdue ▪

If somebody were to gaze down at Coffen's particular subdivision from the great subdivision in the sky, it would be shaped like a capital Y. Currently, he hobbles from the main gate, down at the bottom of the Y and up toward the fork, where he'll veer left to reach Schumann's—his own light gray palace much farther down the same street.

"Coffen?" a voice says.

Bob limps in the middle of the road. There's blood dripping from his brow. He'd been so mired in savage thoughts that he hadn't heard the whir of an electric car coming up next to him.

"Hey, Westbrook," says Bob.

"What's the other guy look like?"

"Schumann."

"Wish I looked like Schumann."

"No, it actually was Schumann."

"He kicked your ass?"

"He ran me off the road. I'm going to kick his ass now."

Westbrook, unlike Schumann, can keep his vehicle at a steady speed, chugging next to Coffen down the darkened block. "You'll be massacred," Westbrook says.

"That's why we play the game."

"What game?"

"Purdue versus Notre Dame."

"Which one are you in this metaphor?" asks Westbrook.

"I'm Purdue. I'm the underdog."

"At least let me drive you to his house. You look like a hammered turd."

The two men near the Y's fork. "I have to do this on my own, Westbrook. If our paths should cross again, we'll toast to my victory."

"Our paths have to cross again. You still have my tent poles, remember?"

And with that, Westbrook speeds off. Coffen's solitary limp powers on.

■ ■ ■

Bob stands in front of château Schumann, weighing what he should do next. Does he ring the doorbell? Does he hunt for an open window? He hadn't really formulated any kind of plan, per se, as he lurched here. He felt like he'd know what had to be done once he arrived, inspiration striking as he stood on Schumann's green lawn. But really, the longer he hovers on the grass, he's losing some of his anger, his gall. Maybe he should just go home. Maybe he should err on the side of caution. Maybe he should go lick his wounds and try again tomorrow.

A meteorologist might call the conditions *an unusually warm night.*

If Bob had built this, if this current scenario were one of Coffen's video games, then this would be the final level. You won the whole thing if you conquered the neighborhood bane. You got fifty thousand bonus points if you decapitated him. You were labeled the "Subdivision Badass." The surviving neighborhood dads basked in your splendor at the barbecues, their wives all randy for you, swooning each time the winner, Bob Coffen, came by the house returning tent poles.

This isn't a video game, though. Unfortunately not. This is Bob Coffen fresh off falling from his bike, almost being rammed into the oleanders. This is Bob nursing a suspect clavicle and ribs from landing on the plock. This is Bob deciding to swallow another snort of pride and limp home defeated.

Yet right as he's about to surrender, there's a noise coming from inside Schumann's house. This is a noise Bob knows.

Screechy.

Mewling.

High-pitched.

It's bagpipes.

Yup, those are bagpipes coming from Schumann's.

And the spot of pride-swallowing that has been slowly working its way down Coffen's esophagus gets thwarted, deemed irrelevant. He can't go home. No way. He can't pretend that this never happened, Schumann leaving him in the street like roadkill.

These brash bagpipes push Coffen to retaliate. Here he is bleeding on the grass. Here he is bleeding and Schumann is in there merrily bagpiping songs for his family? Here Bob is feeling so alone in his life, feeling so separated from his own wife and kids, and the Schumanns are happily huddled by the hearth appreciating a bagpipe recital? And why had it been so easy for Schumann to abandon Bob in the street back there? Why was it so easy for people to abandon Bob Coffen? First his father had walked out, then the few girlfriends he had throughout his twenties, and now he and Jane had wilted into the ultimate cliché—a sexless marriage. They had a life much like the subdivision itself: walled off from everything, even each other.

All these things inspire an elegant gush of rage in Coffen. He notices an American flag that hangs from a silly stick outside the château, and he thinks that maybe he can indeed think about this as a video game—maybe the hero can snatch the skinny flagpole. Maybe he can position himself in front of the huge picture window in Schumann's living room—maybe this hero can pull back his arm to heave the patriotic javelin, the American flag whipping behind it—maybe Bob Coffen is in fact this hero.

He feels the bruised clavicle burn even though he's using the opposite arm to throw the javelin, not that the agony much matters, no way, because nothing's going to keep Coffen from doing this.

He watches the javelin sail, the flag waggling behind it.

Bob watches and admires his toss as it glides toward the window.

Watches its trajectory and thinks: *The HOA will not be impressed with what's transpiring on one of its hallowed lawns. Bob thinks, I might be stepping in some serious shit, but oh boy, does sticking up for myself feel good.*

Yes, if this were a video game, the picture window explodes!

Sure, if this were a video game, Bob's well on his way to winning.

But in Coffen's reality, his aim isn't such great shakes. His javelin misses the huge picture window. Misses it badly. His heave is over near the front door and knocks off a flowerpot that's suspended from a support beam. It shatters on the porch.

The sounds of breaking terra-cotta halt Schumann's bagpipe recital. Commotion in the douche's lair. Footsteps stomping, dead bolt turning, and any second Coffen will hear a stampede through the door, and the featured brawl can commence, pitting the underdog versus Notre Dame.

Schumann opens the front door, holding his bagpipes, spies Coffen out on the lawn. He yells back into the house for his wife and kids to stay put, he'll handle this. *It's only Bob.* Then he says in a calm voice, "Your head's bleeding pretty good."

Coffen nods.

"Look," Schumann says, "let's not make things any worse."

"You can't smear me into the oleanders."

"Seriously, your head is pouring blood."

"And my shoulder's hurt, too."

"I'll take you to the hospital."

Coffen stares at the bagpipes, limp in Schumann's arms like a sleeping toddler. Bob wipes some blood from his face and asks, "What song were you playing before?"

"Huh?"

"What song was that?"

"The fight song of my alma mater. Called 'Hail Purdue.'"

"A fight song?"

"Our call to arms."

Having fought for something—having fought for himself—Bob feels like he needs to hear the song in its entirety. He fancies himself victorious in this situation with Schumann, despite the mangled bicycle, the bleeding head—despite the fact he's only hours removed from somebody honoring him with a plock, probably the most malicious prize ever designed. Always midnight. Always lying about how much time has gotten away from him. Always Robert.

"Before we go to the hospital, will you fire it up again?" Coffen says.

"Why?"

"I want to hear the song."

Schumann looks momentarily confused, then shrugs.

He gets the bagpipes going, those gigantic, funereal squawks. Coffen stands on the lawn listening to "Hail Purdue" coat the whole subdivision in celebration. For some reason, Coffen has brought his hand up and placed it over his heart like he's pledging allegiance to something.

■ Tough-love life coach ■

Bob initially hated how the bagpipes squawked, but soon the sounds transform into the most beautiful music ever, and Coffen is mesmerized, burrowing deep into the fight song's melody. He's heard people talk about experiencing things so perfect, so sating, that they feel they can die happy right then. Finally, he understands the meaning of such righteous hyperbole. It's a moment nude of any other details, life freezing momentarily—much like the plock's hands—and it's only Bob, inside the fight song, finding solace in the idea he can stand up for himself. Sounds simple, easy, obvious to a certain kind of person: Of course you should stand up for yourself; you're supposed to do that. But for somebody emotionally programmed with a three-thousand-pound inferiority complex, like Coffen, this act of resistance is a major coup.

Being imbedded inside "Hail Purdue" doesn't last long, though. Before Schumann launches into the fight song's final chorus—*Bam! Knock! Splat!*—down Coffen crashes onto the lawn, out cold, hand falling from his heart.

Next thing Bob sees is Schumann's missus hovering over him, saying, "We can rule out death because I think he's breathing. Are you breathing? I think I see him breathing probably."

"I'm not," Coffen says.

"Not breathing?"

"Not dead."

"Obviously," she says, "we're in the midst of conversing."

Next thing Coffen remembers after that is being in the SUV with Schumann, driving down the main road in the subdivision.

"Stay with me, muchacho. Schumann shall save the day."

"I don't need you to save my day."

"I want to save your day."

"Do you know I've fantasized for years about hurting you?" Bob asks.

"That's what I'm talking about!" Schumann says, taking his hands off the wheel and clapping a few times—slow, awestruck applause. "I love it! Who would have thought you had violence in you. I feel a new kinship to you, Coffen. Dare I say I like you after you threw that flagpole and admitted you want to kick my ass! You're a possessed warrior tonight. 'In the zone,' as Coach used to say. Honestly, I see you in a whole new light. One that makes me deeply respect you. I have a business proposition, my friend."

"We aren't friends," says Coffen.

"I think we might be now."

"You're always making fun of me at our block parties."

"It's nothing personal. Comic relief helps everyone relax at those things."

"I don't find it particularly relaxing when everybody thinks I'm a pussy."

"Don't be so thin-skinned."

"You told the guys I couldn't play touch football because of my yeast infection," says Coffen.

Schumann tries to repress a giggle, but it slips out. "That's your standard locker room razz."

"This isn't a locker room. This is real life."

"Real life is a gigantic locker room, Coffen," he says, laughing harder.

They've turned out of their subdivision, driving down the road with the oleander. Coffen sees his wrecked bike, his rucksack, and says, "Pull over."

"Why?"

"I need my plock."

"That's not a word."

"I need my plock to remind me not to give up another decade."

"Maybe your tongue is swelling from injury and I can't decipher your slurred speech."

"I'll show you."

Schumann pulls the SUV into the bike lane and Coffen hops out, retrieves his newly received anniversary present, jumps back in the vehicle.

"Oh, you meant 'clock,'" Schumann says.

"No, plock."

"Man, you really hit your head hard."

"You hit my head hard. You tried to ram me with your car, prick."

"Look, I shouldn't have run you toward that oleander."

"You think?"

"It's my damn competitive streak. I want to win the whole world."

"You could have seriously injured me."

"Coach used to say I take things too far."

"He's right."

"He used to punish me after practice, and you should,

too. It's the only way I learn. Do you want to ram me with my car so we're even?"

"What?"

"Then we'd be fair and square, except technically I never rammed you with my car. Technically, I only *almost* rammed you. But I can overlook this inconsistency. I can take one ramming for our team. Don't go faster than my speed from earlier—seven miles per hour."

"You're saying I can hit you with this SUV right now?"

"Only if you want to. There's no obligation. If you don't feel up to it, I'm totally fine with that."

"No," Bob says. "I'd like very much to hit you with a car."

"And then we're even."

"Why would you do this?"

"Psycho Schumann's not doing anything. You're doing something." Schumann opens his door. He walks in front of the SUV, stops about fifteen feet down the road.

Coffen crawls over the console and into the driver's seat, plock riding shotgun.

He looks at Schumann standing out there in the headlights.

Looks and thinks about how rare it is when a fantasy comes true: Bob's secret yearnings to inflict pain on his subdivision foe are about to be realized.

He revs the engine.

"I am not afraid of anything," Schumann says. "I'd take a grizzly bear's temperature rectally. I'd tickle Sasquatch's ass with a feather."

"You ready?" Bob asks.

"Are you ready?"

"I can't wait," says Coffen.

He means it—or really, Bob *wants* to mean it. A certain

part of Coffen is excited by the impending violence, but unfortunately, that faction of his psyche is outweighed by a more empathic caucus, a body of voices all whispering the same thing in his head: *You can't do this. No matter what, this is a road too low for you. Don't go down to this disgusting level.*

"Hut, hut, hike!" Schumann says, eyes closed, arms flexed.

But the SUV doesn't move, continuing to idle.

"I can't do it," Bob says.

"What?" Schumann says, his eyes still closed.

"I can't ram you, even though I really want to ram you."

"Why can't you?"

"I'm not insane."

Schumann lopes back to the driver's door; Coffen climbs back over into the passenger seat, holds the plock in his lap. Schumann starts driving and says, "I think I can coach you, Coffen."

"How's that?"

"Imagine you're on a football team and you get a new special teammate. Imagine that every player on the opposing team is not on steroids, and they are sort of weaklings, staggering around and not really doing very good out on the field. And this new special teammate of yours is on steroids and sculpted like a Roman statue and having him on your team is going to guarantee a stampede into the playoffs. Does this sound like the kind of teammate you might want on your side?"

Bob doesn't respond. He should've hit him with the car.

Schumann continues, "What I'm saying is that I'm like your new teammate."

"What are you getting at?"

"You see this all the time in sports," Schumann says. "Heated competitors in one season get swapped onto the same team the next, and once teammates, they transcend any grudges of yore."

"Yore?"

"It means things that happened in the past."

"I know what it means," Coffen says.

"So what I'm saying is, I can help you. I know lots of things that maybe might help somebody like you."

"Like what?"

"I can coach you to always act like the guy who threw that flagpole at my house. Not the pansy you usually are. You'll always be a fearless warrior."

Schumann looks at Coffen, awaiting acknowledgment, but Bob doesn't say shit, the clang in his brain getting worse. Words are far from his lips, locked behind some sort of window painted shut. Coffen will soon find out that a concussion is the culprit, but maybe it's other things, too: Maybe it's this new way Schumann speaks to him—with, what, respect? Deference? Equality? Bob's not quite sure, only knows that he digs it.

"How's your head?" Schumann asks. "Your eyes aren't focusing, I don't think."

Bob sees the inherent merits in Schumann's suggestion: Having him as a kind of tough-love life coach will not only take some pressure off, it might also earn a few bonus points at the neighborhood barbecues, jealous fathers wondering when these two kissed and made up, now trotting around like long-lost chums. Plus, Jane has always raved about Bev Schumann, and maybe now the couples can go out for paella.

Bob extends his hand out toward Schumann for a shake and says, "You want to be my life coach?"

"I don't think that's exactly what I said."

"Can you teach me to be manlier? Like Gotthorm?"

"Who's Gotthorm?"

"Never mind," says Bob. "I don't want to talk about him. I don't want to be pushed around anymore."

"I can definitely help with that," Schumann says. "Training starts now. Let's stop for some pizza on the way home from the ER. Demand that I pay for it."

"Buy the pizza, please."

"A kindergartener can be scarier than that."

Bob pauses for a couple seconds, then screams, "You're going to buy me a pizza. And there will be several expensive toppings."

A smiling, hand-shaking Schumann says, "That's the spirit."

"And cancel any plans you might have for Friday. You're chauffeuring Jane and me to a magic show."

▪ Scroo Dat Pooch ▪

Dumper Games is decorated like a dignified day care. That's all the rage with greedy corporations these days, disguising themselves as elaborate romper rooms with Ping-Pong, billiard, and foosball tables, entire walls of vintage video games from the 1980s, kegs of microbrewed ale available whenever an employee fancies a pint. None of the young workers wear shoes, all lollygagging around in argyle socks.

Malcolm Dumper, wearing his patented #99 Gretzky uni, invites Bob and his team into the conference room to plop down on one of the beanbags (of course, there's no conference table or regular chairs in the conference room) and brainstorm. To powwow. To spitball ideas. To come up with a game so good it will boomerang DG back to its glory days. Specifically, Dumper wants this new game to corner the highly desirable and highly stunted eighteen-to-thirty-four-year-old male demographic: a land where scatology is king, a sad, lonely world where a certain segment of guys game and game and game their lives away, only taking breaks to jerk off or eat a Hot Pocket. And then quickly back to gaming. And then maybe another jerk. Another Pocket. Ad infinitum . . .

Once everybody takes a seat on a beanbag, as is his tradition, Dumper launches these brainstorms with a speech, macerating his metaphors to pulp: "The Dumper family needs to make some immediate changes to our catalog and make them fast. Imagine Dumper as a massive ship. This ship of ours needs to bore full speed ahead to generate revenue, yet it also needs to do a 180-degree about-face to get away from the boring titles we've already put out this year. Of course, no sailing vessel can do these two contradictory things at once. But we have to try to accomplish them, or who knows how long our doors will be open. Am I saying there's imminent door closage? Not exactly. But the Great One is saying that our doors might get antsy to slam if we don't start raking in some serious bacon."

"Are you talking about buying a company yacht?" the mouth-breather says. He's almost half Coffen's age, has only worked at DG for eight months. Bob can't wait until he gets fired, pursues an industry more suited to his talents, say a tenured position as the chief mouth-breathing lackey at a sleep apnea clinic. "For, like, fishing trips?"

"The Great One is talking about us. I'm talking about us taking the eighteen-to-thirty-four-year-old male demo and bouncing it on our knee and entertaining them with something edgier than they've ever imagined. And you're the team to do it. So dazzle me with your pitches. Let me wet my beak on your fantastic ideas. Let me douse my beak. Submerge it underwater, deeper than the *Titanic*."

"What about a stoner's quest," says the mouth-breather, "in which a guy goes on a journey to find the perfect bong? Early levels give him pretty good bongs—nice draw, a properly placed carb—but each new level the bongs grow by a foot. The last level he can get a ten-footer. That's like the Sistine Chapel for bong aficionados."

"You suggest that same idea at every meeting," Dumper

says, his humungous tongue safely stowed in his mouth, alerting everyone that he's not impressed.

"I'm pretty sure I nailed the pitch this time," the mouth-breather says.

"These drug ideas are a different demo. Teens. Maybe preteens."

"Bongs never go out of style, like turtlenecks."

"Dude, turtlenecks are completely out of style," another young team member says to the mouth-breather.

"Focus," says Dumper. "Please. Shock me with your edginess. Let's get back to our rightful Disemboweler throne."

Coffen had masterminded the whole Disemboweler franchise: Disemboweler I: Flesh for Breakfast; Disemboweler II: Tasty Comrades; Disemboweler III: Zombie Happy Hour; Disemboweler IV: Let's Get Bloody! The first game had been Bob's breakthrough success, and he built it back before computer advancements made it so simple to design games. Coffen did this before all the drag-and-drop technologies simplified the process so any novice could put a half-assed game together. He learned the trade back in a dark age when, god forbid, humans had to do the coding themselves. He constructed entire ecosystems from his imagination, dreamed up elaborate, sinister narratives for his characters. Bob saw this creation as pure beauty, on the same level as writing a sonata or chiseling a sculpture from a slab of marble. But at a certain point, technology ruined it for Coffen. Talent didn't matter if any idiot could cut and paste stock images, drag them into a prefab world, and pass that schlock off as a game. His job, once ripe with art and self-expression, was spoiled. The sonatas were silent. The marble was safe.

Now Dumper says, "Let's get our company back to being the big men on campus."

"And one woman," the only woman on our team says.

"Of course," Dumper says. "Beaucoup apologies. Anybody have another idea?"

A normally quiet team member launches into his pitch: "What about this gem: a game called Hey, That's My Meth Lab! You'll be a rival speed dealer trying to blow up all of your competitors' meth labs."

"How would you win that game?" the mouth-breather says, no doubt feeling competitive since his suggestion also covered narcotics territory.

"Once everybody's buying your crank, you are crowned the champion of meth. You are the sultan of amphetamines."

"No more ideas that have to do with drugs, okay?" Dumper says. "Next time we brainstorm like this, there will be a moratorium on illicit substances. Anybody else?" Dumper looks more and more like he's regretting asking this team to think in an impromptu way.

Another team member quickly seizes the moment to showcase his immense potential for design: "Everyone I know—and I'm right smack in the heart of the demo we're discussing—loves conspiracy theories. So what if we built a game that's like a puzzle to solve an ancient riddle about how extraterrestrials aren't extra at all. They're us; they're terrestrials. We are all aliens, bro! Extraterrestrials are terrestrials and vice versa. Can you imagine? People would wig out!"

"Is that what 'terrestrial' means? It means human?" the mouth-breather says.

The showcaser continues: "Yeah, humans. Us. We are us, but we are also aliens. We're all god's terrestrials. It's like a metaphor for racism."

"And why would your demo want to play a metaphor for racism?" Dumper asks.

"Because racism metaphors don't have to be boring. There will be kickass explosions and topless ladies, sir. Lasers. Flying, time-traveling Cadillacs. If it has the potential to be awesome, it will be a highlighted component of the game. No questions asked."

"So what's the conspiracy theory exactly?"

"We're aliens! What's more of a conspiracy than finding out you're something other than what you thought you were?"

"It's the best bad idea so far," says Dumper.

"We're all something other than what we thought we'd be," Coffen says.

Everybody stares at him.

Dumper says, "So you like the terrestrial idea then, Coffen?"

"I hate the idea."

"Me, too," Dumper says. "Have you got anything that might impress the Great One? Can you astound me like you used to do back in the good old Disemboweler days?"

All of us in this room are imbeciles, Bob thinks, *working for a man-boy in a Gretzky sweater. He's our pimp. He profits on laying our imaginations on their backs or bending them over a barrel and banging them from behind or reverse-cowgirling our imaginations until he gets all he wants, leaving them spent and soiled, discarded like losing lottery tickets.*

Coffen decides to defend his imagination's honor by pointing out to all in attendance how vapid Dumper is: The Great One wants something to tickle the lowest common denominator? Bongs and meth labs be damned. This meeting is about to hit the basement. The denominator at the center of the earth.

"Bestiality," Coffen says.

"What now?" Dumper asks.

"What's edgier than bestiality? I could see this becoming a cult classic. Do you know how many drugged-up undergrads would love this?"

The team starts tittering.

After several seconds, Dumper says, "How would it work?"

"May I stand up to demonstrate?" Bob asks.

"Of course," Malcolm Dumper says, and here comes his humungous tongue, slowly slithering out.

It takes Bob about ten seconds to jimmy his weight off of the beanbag. He's still pretty woozy, only about twelve hours removed from the oleander incident. Jane had tried to talk him into taking the day off, but he'd insisted on coming to work. Why had he fought her to come here? For this? For beanbags? For bestiality?

Coffen is finally standing up. His imagination needs a neighborhood watch with Dumper around, a rape whistle.

"It would be a game," Bob says, "without any handset controls. No, a game of this transgressive magnitude would need to work with user movements. We've seen Wii games where a user's body movements can translate to the screen, the character in the game mimicking what the user is doing at home. This title would require that sort of technology. It would be an advancement for us in many ways, as we've never built anything in this style."

Bob holds his hands out, waist high, pretending that somebody—or some animal—is positioned in front of him, bent over. Then Coffen begins maniacally thrusting his hips in a coital-inspired manner. He strikes a rather rollicking pace with his thrusts and keeps them up while continuing the pitch.

"I imagine a game where the character meanders the mean streets trying to have sex with every stray dog he can find. As the game progresses, soon the avatar has to prowl into the homes of private citizens to defile man's best friend. Finally, for the grand finale, the sneaky, horny, maladjusted avatar must evade Secret Service and screw the president's dog right in the Oval Office."

Coffen gets winded as he continues to give the business to the imaginary dog while talking.

"Dude, that's disgusting," the mouth-breather says, smiling, "and I would play it all day, every day, until I died."

"What about the rest of you?" Dumper asks the remaining team members.

"I'd totally play that!"

"It's awesome!"

"My friends are gonna love this filth!"

"What's it called, Coffen?"

Bob grins, plunges aimlessly into the invisible pet. "Scroo Dat Pooch," he calls out, and the juniors clap.

One of them says, "Dude is a genius."

"He was just hibernatin' since Disemboweler."

Another: "It's like watching da Vinci paint a masterpiece."

"The bestiality *Mona Lisa*!"

"Jesus, stop gyrating like that," Dumper says to Bob.

Bob concludes his coital parade, sags back down into his beanbag. His head hurts. It feels good to make a mockery of this, good to suggest something so far over the line that despite the enthusiasm of the juniors, Dumper has no choice but to say no chance in hell. Edgy's one thing, but this idea is too taboo.

But apparently, there is chance in hell.

Apparently, Coffen hasn't been making a mockery of

anything, at least not to the only person whose opinion on the subject matters: the Great One. Dumper reels his tongue back in his mouth, says, "Build a test level, Bob. I want to see how it plays."

"Are you sure?" Coffen says.

"I'm not sure. But I'm window-shopping, snooping in the store. Now grab the bull by the horns and make the final sale. Can you do that for me?"

"I can try."

"DG needs this. Our doors are getting itchy trigger fingers for some closage. Don't let that happen. Now say it with some enthusiasm: Can you make the final sale to this window-shopper and appease our moody doors?"

"Bob is me," Bob says, dejected—he can't even sabotage his job correctly.

"Scroo Dat Pooch," Dumper says. "Now that's funny. Sick, but funny. No guarantees we'll continue with it, but I'd like to see what it looks like. This might be a new direction not only for DG, but your titles, Coffen. You've never done anything comic before. This might be your renaissance."

"That's a reasonable suggestion," says Bob.

"Get something rough together for next Monday's status meeting."

"That's not much time."

"It's not. But you're a pro's pro. Make it happen."

Dumper and the juniors skedaddle from the conference room, leaving Bob alone on his beanbag. He stays like that for some time.

▪ Fluorescent orange ▪

Bob's time of beanbag contemplation is interrupted when he sees his wife's face pressed up against the glass of the conference room. Jane's braids are wet; she must have come here straight from the high-priced gym where she trains. She's working toward breaking the world record for treading water, which is currently at eighty-five hours. Her personal best is fifty-nine hours straight.

She eyeballs Bob through the glass. There's something unusual about her expression that Coffen can't exactly get a bead on. He assumes it's a face much like the Native Americans must have worn toward the early Pilgrims: curiosity and apprehension and pity.

Seeing Jane in an office environment reminds Bob of where they'd first met. He worked at a company building web-platform games, ones to be downloaded and installed locally on users' hard drives. She worked in the customer service department. Bob made up all kinds of asinine reasons to trundle over to CS and bug her. He'd feign interest in the customers' problems solely to talk to her, hoping to grow the confidence to ask her out.

He waited a long time for that mysterious confidence to swell, but it never did. He was too much of a pussy.

The other guys on his team happily reminded him that he should let it go, no chance in hell he'd ever ask, and even if he did, what was the probability of Jane wanting to date Bob? In the end, he decided to build her something, knew that if he had a shot with her it would be in a different world than this one. He worked round the clock for three days building it and then emailed her the zipped files with instructions for how to install the HTML on her system to get into this new world he'd constructed for them.

The email only said: *Jane, please meet me in here tonight at 10:30.*

He sat at home, slugging Coke from a two-liter, and waiting like an antsy child who needs to take a leak but is stuck in the backseat of the family sedan. Waiting and feeling stupid for doing all this. She wasn't going to show. Why would she show? No doubt she could do better than a bloated coder.

It was 10:33.

On his computer screen, Bob's avatar stood alone in the world he'd built. He designed the avatar to look like himself, save for a smaller waistline. The avatar was on the left-hand side of the screen, standing next to an elaborate maze. There was an Italian restaurant on the other side of it.

At 10:35 Coffen finished the two-liter of soda, which means he consumed the whole thing in a little over twenty minutes. His kidneys were not thrilled with the carbonated poison pumping through them.

I'll wait until 10:45, Bob thought. *And if that's not enough time for her, I'll wait until five in the morning, but not a minute longer!*

It didn't come to that.

At 10:39, Jane's avatar popped onto the screen: It was a spitting image of her. The braids on her head. The yellow cardigan she always wore to the office. The black-rimmed glasses.

I'm here! her avatar said in a chat bubble. *Sorry I'm late. Traffic on the highway was out of hand! Bumper to bumper.* ☺

Was there an overturned big rig blocking your path?

Toxic chemical spill.

I hope its noxious fumes didn't infect you with a secret government-cultivated disease.

That's a sweet thing to say.

I'm a gentleman.

Where are we?

We're on a date. Are you hungry?

Starved!

Let's go dig in.

Their avatars entered the maze. It took about ten minutes for them to stumble through it, making small talk the whole time, finally arriving at the restaurant. Once their avatars touched the shape of the restaurant's exterior, the background changed. Now they were inside the restaurant, sitting at a table.

Do you like grilled calamari? Bob's avatar said. *The chef here is known for it.*

When I was a little girl, a two-ton squid escaped from the zoo. It crawled in my window and hid under my bed. I kept it alive on saltwater taffy.

That squid is lucky it found you.

It's a blessing and a curse, though. Now every single squid that escapes the ocean tries to track me down. It's a headache.

LOL!

A robust, tan, mustachioed man came and took their order. Soon steaming piles of food appeared on their table. The avatars ate everything up.

After the meal, they sat at the table smoking cigarettes.

Jane said, *I like how these cigarettes don't make my breath bad.*

Your breath is superb.

You're a smooth talker in this place, aren't you?

No, I just like you.

I didn't know you wanted to ask me out.

Bob's avatar tamped out his cigarette. *I'm shy.*

Me too. But you don't need to be shy around me. I like you.

You do?

Everybody at work does! You build the best games. I mean, look where we are right now!. You're amazing.

Thanks for meeting me here tonight.

Any time! I'm going to go get some sleep, Jane said. *I have a CS meeting at eight tomorrow. Will you miss me until we're at work together?*

Of course.

Make sure and give the waiter a big tip. He did a phenomenal job. ☺ Bye, Bob! Thanks for doing this for me.

Hold on. My credit card was rejected. Do you have any traveler's checks or something to pay the bill?

LMAO

Good night, Jane.

XOXO

The next day at work, there was a piece of saltwater taffy sitting next to Bob's keyboard when he got there. He couldn't decide if he wanted to eat it or keep it forever. Then a chat window popped up on Coffen's screen. It was Jane.

Want to go out for lunch? I'm in the mood for calamari ☺
I know a great place, said Bob.

I mean, real calamari. Let's me and you go out to lunch together.

Awesome!

And that was it. They had lunch. Then they had more meals. Nobody in the office could believe it. None of the other programmers understood how or why Jane had chosen Bob, and frankly Coffen didn't much understand it himself. But he didn't care. No reason to question such luck.

Then after about ten dates, they kissed. Slowly, they fell in love. Slowly, they decided to get married and have kids.

And now, here Bob is, staring at her through the glass.

Jane waves and Bob clumsily peels himself off the beanbag, meets her in the doorway. They do not kiss. She smells of chlorine, which turns him on: She used to be so horny after exercise. Now its scent makes Coffen wince—when did they dissipate into their kids' chaperones?

She says, "You're wearing your sad face, Mister Grumbles."

"You wouldn't believe what game I have to build next. Humiliating. I don't want to talk about it. How was your tread? How many hours did you do this morning?"

"Not that many. I'm tapering off before I make a run at the record again on Monday."

"Oh, I thought that was next Monday."

"You can't fit my record attempt into your grumbly brain?"

"Sorry."

"It's this Monday. This is exactly the behavior that I need to talk to you about."

"Is everything okay?"

"Would I be here if everything was okay?"

■ ■ ■

It's a quick walk across the street to the corporate café. Their town is a patchwork of subdivisions and strip malls and office parks. It's the kind of suburb that had such a quick population influx after the dot-com boom that its city planning had been slapdash, nonsensical. Chain stores popped up quicker than saloons in frontier towns. Competing businesses were in dangerous proximity to one another: A bagel and sandwich shop could be right next store to a sandwich and salad shop, which could be right next to a sandwich and coffee shop. That last one is where the Coffens walk into now.

"What kind of coffee would you like?" asks Bob.

"I had a very interesting conversation this morning with Aubrey Westbrook," Jane says.

"How is she?"

"Is it true?"

"I don't know what we're talking about."

"Didn't you chat with her husband last night?" Jane asks, and of course Bob had, limping in the road, regaling Westbrook of Coffen's immediate itinerary: going to Schumann's and locking horns with the heavy favorite.

The barista asks the Coffens, "What can I do to make your day even better?"

"Black coffee for me," Bob says, "and a latte for the lady."

"I don't want anything," Jane says. "Watching my dairy before the big tread."

"What kind of black coffee would you like?" the barista asks. "We have six house coffees. We feature ethically cultivated coffees from around the globe. We have blends from Rwanda, Colombia, Venezuela, Brazil, Uganda, and the Malay Archipelago."

"I take it black."

"Do you enjoy flavors of fresh-squeezed grapefruit? Because that would be the Rwandan blend."

"Jesus, just pour him whatever is your favorite," Jane says.

The barista looks disappointed but does as she's told, setting the steaming mug in front of him on the counter.

"Which one did you go with?" Bob asks the barista, playing good cop to Jane's brusque one.

"Rwandan."

He smells the coffee and says, "You're right: fresh-squeezed grapefruit."

The Coffens pay and move to a table. A Muzak version of Nirvana's "Smells Like Teen Spirit" trickles from hidden speakers. It had been one of Bob's favorite songs, back when he was in high school, and now it was demoted to the barbiturate of background noise. *It happens to us all,* Bob thinks—*we age and lose our relevance, even rock stars.*

The table is small and circular and lacquered into its top is the iconic picture of King Kong atop the Empire State Building, swatting at airplanes.

"So Aubrey told me a confusing story about last night," Jane says. "You did run into her husband, right?"

"I did. We still have their tent poles."

"She said you told him that Schumann ran you off the road."

"I'd totally forgotten we even borrowed their tent poles."

"You told me you fell off your bike and Schumann drove you to the hospital."

"I might have left out the beginning." Bob sticks his tongue in his coffee—still too hot. He looks down at King Kong instead.

"So you lied to me."

"If you think omission is lying."

"Everyone thinks omission is lying."

"I didn't know how to tell you the truth. It's embarrassing."

"Do you remember when I caught you jerking off last week with the chips?" Jane's face goes from its earlier contortion—the appropriated curiosity and apprehension and pity lifted from the Native Americans—and morphs into flat-out disgust. "Are you saying this is more embarrassing than that?"

A week ago Tuesday: Coffen had been minding his own tawdry business on the Internet—wife and kids sleeping the night away. He was another half-drunken, lonely, sad, suburban father sitting in his study, inappropriately conducting fevered searches re the shaving habits of certain coeds who were okay with strangers witnessing the upkeep of their nether regions. Coffen gawked and Googled and swigged vodka on the rocks from a sweating tumbler and munched nacho cheese Doritos, and a rhythm developed between these motions—gawking, Googling, slurping, munching. It was the vodka that presented the first problem piece of the puzzle. See, in his haste and enthusiasm Coffen wasn't paying attention to the condensation from the glass, how it made his fingers moist, how with the next clumsy dip of his hand into the Doritos bag, the orange dust plastered itself to it. Under normal circumstances, he would have identified the vibrant sticking orange dust and properly cleaned it off, but he wasn't exactly in his right mind, a combustion slowly stoking in his body, and as the scene built to its dejected ending, he dropped his pants and latched his phallus in his fist and the vibrant, gummy orange dust transferred and stuck to it like fluorescent sawdust.

Meanwhile, Jane, thirsty, awakened, and wondering why Coffen hadn't come to bed, burst into his office and observed the scene for herself—Bob yanking sadly, his prick bright orange.

Shame rained on him immediately. Coffen thought: *Two people can know each other so well and yet there are always new ways to disappoint your partner, disappoint yourself.*

He quickly pulled up his pants and pushed his fluorescent orange penis inside.

"Those chips are supposed to be for the kids," Jane said, and walked out.

Now Bob says, "It's a different kind of embarrassing, but I'll tell you if that's what you want." Coffen tells her another pared-down version of the truth, one that contains more of the crucial plot points than the first iteration he'd shared, yet it still isn't entirely true: In this new remix, Coffen and Schumann were having a good-humored competition, a couple blokes fooling around on their way home, horseplay between subdivision friends that unfortunately didn't end the way either had hoped or expected or wanted.

"Why would you agree to race a car on a bicycle?" she asks with the same judgmental look she'd given Bob after seeing him fluorescent orange. It's as though he's covered in the artificial dust as they sit in the café.

"Boys will be boys," Bob says.

"Your gender is ridiculous."

"Yes, we are."

"But I'm glad you're okay."

It's the closest thing to affection she's said to him lately, and it makes Bob happy to hear her express gladness that he's all right. (Last night, after returning from the ER, Jane seemed like the whole episode was inconvenient, didn't express any worry for Bob at all.) He'll take what he can get, stares down at the lacquered King Kong, frozen there, stuck in mid-swat. "Tell me about your morning tread. Are you all ready to go for the world record? Does Gotthorm think you're ready?"

"Well, that's actually what I want to talk with you about," she says.

Gotthorm is her water-treading coach. He played goalie on the Norwegian water polo team in the 1984 Olympics, and to see him today, you'd think he could still leap in the pool and tussle with the youngsters. Or hop over to the next fjord and burn and steal whatever tickles his plundering fancy.

Gotthorm always stands by the pool in only his red Speedo, encouraging Jane, his cock and balls like assistant coaches poking through the flimsy suit. Coffen himself can't help but stare at Gotthorm's bulge on the days he stops by Jane's training sessions to show his support. It's not the size of the bulge. No obscene mound distends the Speedo. It's the nakedness, the proximity of the bulge. How from Jane's vantage point in the pool, she has to stare up at it for hours at a time, treading water there—a bulge on a pedestal, if you will. In fact, Coffen sometimes can't help but assume the worst: Gotthorm, Jane, and his bulge, the three of them someday riding off into the sunset together.

"Talk to me about what?" Bob asks, slurping his coffee.

"We think that maybe the reason I cramped up the last time I went for the record is that my mind was too heavy. I was literally weighed down by my mind."

"Your mind literally weighed more?"

"We were thinking that this time my mind needs to be free. Totally lithe. It has to weigh less than a single scale from a fish."

"How does one diet her brain weight?" Bob asks, feeling the threat of laughter. This is classic Gotthorm. He talks about treading water in a new age way that makes Coffen want to puke. Her brain is literally too heavy with thoughts, weighs her down, drags her to the bottom. Yup, that's obviously the problem.

"We're not sure you should be there this time. I psychically weigh more with you around."

"Thanks."

"That's not meant as a criticism."

"Sucker punch is more like it."

"Bob, you know how much this record means to me. Please. Don't blow this out of proportion. I want to set myself up to succeed. I'm asking for you to help me in a different way this time out. Help me by not being there. I really want the record."

"I mean, there's nothing I can really say. The kids and I will keep our distance."

"Oh, the kids can be there," says Jane. "We think it's best if I see them through the travails of treading for so many hours, so I remember why I'm working so hard. They bring out the best in me. Gotthorm says motherhood is very primal and I'll push myself even harder if I see my children present."

"Is there anyone else besides me who has to stay away?"

"Don't turn this into a 'poor me' thing, Mister Grumbles. Don't do that thing where you feel sorry for yourself and I have to comfort you."

"I will cheer from a distance," Coffen says, simply because there's nothing else he can say. Going over the top with some fuming tirade won't change her mind. He needs to be mature. He knows—or thinks he knows—that she's not trying to hurt his feelings. If this is what gives her the best chance to break the world record, so be it.

Bob had stood by the pool the whole time during her last attempt, only breaking away to use the bathroom. The kids were there for some of the time, too, cheering her on. But it's hard for children to understand the immense achievement of treading water for so long. To them, it's boring. It's hard to watch. But Coffen understood Jane's dedication. He knew how hard she'd worked at it, how she had cramped up, her head spending more and more time under the water, until finally the record attempt had to be called off in the name of safety—it was Bob, not Gotthorm, who held her as she cried that night.

"The world record is eighty-five hours," Jane says. "That's three and a half days. It doesn't sound like such a long time to tread until you're the one bobbing in the pool. Then it feels like your whole life."

"Tell Gotthorm how I used to train with you, treading water as long as I could last. I've always been supportive. He doesn't like me."

"He doesn't understand guys like you. He's like Schumann. They are built to use their bodies. You're not."

Coffen needs to change the subject before, like Kong, he takes one bullet too many and falls to his death. He tries to get it out of his head that Jane wants Gotthorm, tries but it's not working. Why would she choose Bob over a modern-day Viking? He goes with, "Are you excited for Björn the Bereft's magic show on Friday?"

"I hear he's a miracle worker," she says. "But it's more marriage counseling than magic show."

"What made you want to do this in the first place?" Bob asks.

"We made me want to do this," she says.

Coffen retreats to his coffee. He was lying earlier to the barista—he can't smell or taste any grapefruit in the brew. Nirvana's dirge is over. A new song he doesn't recognize starts up. King Kong is frozen for all time. And Bob is covered in fluorescent orange, like a crop duster had targeted him and spackled him in the artificial film. A visual marker for all that he's done wrong, so many mistakes that Jane doesn't want him to cheer her on as she goes for the record. Everybody else on planet earth is welcome, just not Bob.

The Muzak feels like it's getting louder as they sit there in silence.

▪ Looking like a neutered stooge ▪

Bob Coffen stands in his kitchen, waiting for the macaroni to reach the right softness so he can pull the pot off the burner. He sips from a tumbler of vodka and watches his son, Brent, play one of Bob's signature games, Disemboweler IV: Let's Get Bloody!

In this final installment of the franchise, the game chronicles the carnal sojourns of cannibals traipsing through post-apocalyptic America in the hopes of disemboweling the last surviving citizens of this once-proud nation and chomping on their flesh. Right as one lucky cannibal is about to dig in and feast on a victim, they shout to their cohorts, "Let's get bloody!" Once a cannibal croons this signature line, the corresponding graphics never fail to render a scene rich in slaughter, fantastic scribbles of innards and organs.

Brent is good at it, too—perhaps genetically inclined. No normal nine-year-old would be so gifted at these games that readily stump people twice his age. Brent's cannibal dominates the action. In fact, he now rips out another character's larynx and munches away on it, holding the larynx in his hand like an apple.

Brent says to Bob, "Did you see that move, Dad?"

"Good work."

"I'm already on level five."

"Keep it up."

"Benny and Tommy can't get past level two."

"You're a natural."

"Tommy's cat has worms."

"That's no fun."

"Let's get bloody!" Brent says, smiling at Bob, his avatar still choking down the larynx.

Coffen takes another swig of vodka. He's turning his children into house cats: too helpless to fend for themselves outside the subdivision's safe haven. They're going to be easy targets, like him. Their futures are lined with oleanders and plocks.

He spoons out a single piece of macaroni and pops it in his mouth—still a bit crunchy.

Jane enters, dolled to the nines, walks over to a hallway mirror and fusses with her hair, working the wisps back into the elaborate pattern of braids. She has long worn her hair in a system of weaving braids that reminds Coffen of crisscrossing highways. It's something he's always loved about her—the way she's kept this unique hairstyle into middle age, while other subdivision wives look increasingly homogenized.

"Are you sure he's not too young to play that game?" Jane asks.

On-screen, Brent's cannibal repeatedly bashes a citizen's head onto the asphalt, then laps up the stream of synapse stew leaking from the opened skull.

"It's nothing worse than what's online."

"Does that mean he should play it?"

Bob picks up his vodka and has another sip. "Are you having fun?" Coffen says to his son.

"Let's get bloody!" Brent calls over.

"He's enjoying himself," Coffen says.

"He's nine," Jane says.

"It's better we're open with him about the real world, so he feels safe enough to ask us questions later about sex, puberty, drugs . . ."

"Cannibalism," she says.

"Exactly. Nothing is taboo in the Coffen residence." Yet once this posit escapes Coffen's lips, his face changes. Shoulders slump. He's immediately saddened because not even his denial, a normally impenetrable fortress of rationalizations and white lies and blind spots, can offer asylum from the simple fact that almost everything is taboo in the Coffen residence these days.

Luckily, the conversation can't continue because their daughter, Margot, three years older than Brent, comes into the room, scrolling on her iPad's touch screen. Margot looks up and screams to Brent, "Don't miss the teeth upgrade on the next level, or you'll never be able to eat those Navy SEALs."

"I know that," he says.

"You always miss it."

"I do not."

"Margot, can you help me with something?" Coffen asks his daughter, watching her fingers work the iPad.

"I'm hanging with a friend right now, Dad."

Coffen looks around the room. "Who?"

"Ro."

"Where is she?"

"You mean, 'Where are we?'" She shakes her tablet at him, allowing Bob to make out a 3-D representation of the ocean on its screen, two avatars in wet suits, kicking their finned feet. "And the answer is scuba diving at the Great Barrier Reef."

"Why don't you invite her over for real?" Coffen says.

"The Barrier Reef is so much cooler than being here for real," she says.

While Jane continues to manipulate her maze of hair and Margot studies her underwater trek and sort of watches Brent's cannibal feast on a minister, Coffen pulls the pot of macaroni off the heat without tasting it again, dumps it in a colander. Then he pours it back into the pot and stirs in the orangey-cheese powder and milk for the kids' dinner. He slops it into two bowls and stands there drinking vodka.

His mother-in-law, Erma, waddles in. She's five feet and one inch of diabetic rage and immediately belts out, "What's Brent doing?"

Brent is straddling the minister and eating fistfuls of intestines.

"Well, what's he doing?" Erma asks.

Coffen and his mother-in-law aren't exactly bosom chums. There's never been any kind of confrontation or anything because Bob kowtows to her. He tries to communicate with her in simple and direct ways, like this: "He's gaming."

"That game is gross," says Erma, then specifically to Brent, "Turn that off while G-Ma's here."

"Mom, please," Jane says.

"But I've almost beat my all-time high score!" Brent says.

"Fine," Erma says, "beat your all-time high score. Ignore your G-Ma. Pretend your G-Ma's not nearing the end of her life."

"Mom," Jane says.

"What? I won't be around forever. They should appreciate me while I'm still alive."

Brent's avatar is up and off the minister, slowly cornering an Amish-looking woman.

Then there's a tooting car horn out front.

"Schumann's here," Coffen says.

"Schumann?"

"Our chauffeur," Coffen says with a huge smile. "We worked out an agreement for what happened the other night."

The horn toots once more.

"This is weird," Jane says.

"Dad, I thought you hated Schumann," says Margot. "I heard you say he's a douche."

"What's a douche?" Brent asks, outfoxing the Amish lass and now gnawing her thigh to the bone.

Coffen ignores this and asks Jane, "Shall we go, dear?"

She rolls her eyes, goes to get her coat, pats the many braids on her head so as to verify proper geometry. "I guess we shall," she says.

■ ■ ■

"Might I say," Schumann says to Jane, talking with a French accent, "that your sexuality is palpable this evening. If Bob wasn't here, I'd make my play to pleasure you."

He's been laying it on absurdly thick since picking the Coffens up. Talking with that canned French accent, bowing when he opened the car door for Jane, making a big show of it. He's even dressed like a stereotypical chauffeur—black suit, black hat.

Every TV show or movie Coffen has ever seen in which

there are servants, these people know how to keep their traps shut, don't speak unless spoken to, be seen and not heard, etc. So where in his right mind does Schumann think he should be spouting off sexually explicit plans? Bob may not be any kind of chauffeur expert, but come on, this seems like Servitude 101: The help should keep focused on the task at hand.

"Um, thanks," she says.

Both Coffens sit in the SUV's backseat. Bob tries to catch Schumann's eye in the rearview mirror to give him a face that means *Are you seriously being serious right now— palpable sexuality? You're supposed to be a submissive role player, Schumann. Tonight, I'm the quarterback.*

"I don't know about you two," Schumann says, "but my wife and I love a romantic glass of champagne in the park. It's a perfect night for it. I brought a couple champagne flutes and a bottle in case you two were in the mood."

"That does sound nice," Jane says, "but I shouldn't drink any alcohol. I'm going for the treading-water record again on Monday."

But before Coffen can muscle a word in, there's Schumann yammering, "It doesn't sound nice, Jane. It *is* nice. A few sips won't kill you. Coach used to let us have a few beers when we were in training to blow off steam."

She laughs. Is she flirting with him?

"She was talking to me," says Coffen.

"My bad," he says.

"Let's go for it," she says. "Just a few sips."

"That a girl," says Schumann.

■ ■ ■

There are certain things that the blue-ribbon douche might have mastered. And romantic drinks in the park are one, because honestly, this is an idea that never would have occurred to Coffen. Yet look at Jane now, reclining on a blanket in the grassy area as Schumann stands pouring both of them glasses of champagne.

It's dusk. No other people in the small park, which is located inside the subdivision's electric fence. The park is built between the two streets that fork to form the top half of the capital Y. Both Bob and Jane look around, though there's not much to see. Playground far away. Grass and more grass. A couple barbecue pits. A concrete path wending through in great slaloms. There's nothing in the way of distraction—no kids or bills or household maintenance or any other miscellaneous topics that keep Bob's and Jane's minds away from the distance between them. In a sick way, Coffen is happy Schumann is here, drawing so much attention to himself that Bob can bleed into the background a bit, not fixate on the fact he feels uncomfortable.

"Will you be requiring anything else, Monsieur and Madame?" Schumann asks, still showing off with his French accent. He has an oversized backpack slung over one shoulder from which he had produced the champagne and requisite glasses.

"This is splendid," Jane says and smiles. "Thanks for orchestrating all this."

"For a woman of your beauty, this is nothing," he says.

Leave it to Schumann to show Bob up even when he's supposedly his chauffeur. Apparently, even chauffeuring has fine print that Coffen knows nothing about, a mysterious clause in which the driver gets to make the lord of the manor look like a neutered stooge. In the long run, though, Coffen knows that if the smile on Jane's face is any indication, this evening is going really well. Looking like a neutered stooge never felt better.

"And for the cherry on top," says Schumann, futzing with his backpack and ripping out his bagpipes. "Ta-da!"

"Wow," says Jane.

Coffen can't tell whether his wife is being sincere. Bagpipes in the park seems like the kind of thing she would normally mock, but all evidence points to the contrary.

"I'd like to play one of my favorite songs to set the mood," he says.

The last thing on earth Bob wants to hear is Schumann bagpiping a romantic song to set the mood—he's already stealing the spotlight from Bob—yet Coffen knows not to show his true feelings because it's obvious how much Jane wants to hear Schumann perform.

"This song is an oldie but a goody," Schumann says. "I think it accurately captures the sensuous essence of the occasion." He winks at Jane, then looks at Coffen with this face that's saying, *Ahoy, amigo, not sure if you're totally noticing what's going down right now but I'm still 100 percent cooler and better than you, so suck it!*

He shuts his eyes and puffs into the bagpipes' mouthpiece, getting the big squawks going.

▪ Recapture the magic ▪

Imagine a fantastically drab ballroom. Seven square tables have been set up in front of a large stage, each table seating two couples, including Bob and Jane Coffen. Imagine everybody has finished gumming their salmon and parsnip purée and now the overhead lights go out.

Darkness.

Intrigue.

The sound of a recorded heartbeat thumps from the speakers. Loudly at first. It fades until only faintly playing in the background.

The lights go back up, and there are two people standing on the stage, a man and a woman. The man wears a sign on his chest that says SPUTTERING HUSBAND. The woman's sign says ZOMBIE WIFE. They both stagger around the carpeted stage, weaving wildly, like blind people doped on booze without canes or dogs or good Samaritans.

"Who are you?" says Zombie Wife.

"Don't you remember me?" Sputtering Husband asks.

"Oh, yeah, you're that man I've been married to for all these years. You think I'm only a dishwasher and a Laundromat and a baby-making factory."

"And you're the woman who thinks all I do is fart and play fantasy football and you never appreciate the little things I do to help out around the house when I'm not slaving at the office . . ."

"I'm tired of going through the motions," she says.

"I wish there was a way to *recapture the magic* we once possessed," says Sputtering Husband.

They're still staggering around, clomping on the carpeted stage, though now they're both quiet, and in one far corner there's suddenly a puff of smoke that grows in diameter and from it emerges Björn the Bereft. He's wearing a black cape, a black top hat. He is mustachioed.

"Did somebody say '*recapture the magic*'?" Björn says.

"We did! We did!" say Sputtering Husband and Zombie Wife.

"And what about you fine people?" Björn asks the audience. "Are you also here to *recapture the magic?*"

"We're here to *recapture the magic!*" everyone regurgitates in unison.

"I didn't hear that. Why are you here?"

"We're here to *recapture the magic!*"

Coffen looks at Jane while everybody shouts the baited answer back at Björn. She seems to be sincerely participating. Much like the bagpipes back in the park, Bob never would have imagined his wife liking this, and he wonders what it means. If she's changing and he's not, isn't that going to lead to divorce, her fleeing to Gotthorm and his bulge?

"Stand up, please," Björn says, walking toward center stage.

The whole audience does as it's told.

Sputtering Husband and Zombie Wife come close to him, a few feet away. Björn says, "Would any of you like to guess what this stage is made out of?"

Coffen and his tenuously married comrades peek around

with puzzled faces, shrugging shoulders. Most people seem to be eating up the proceedings, but Bob's leaning toward his primordial impulses—to deride this magic show as a cult-in-training: married adults congregating in a ballroom in the hopes a magician will make their marriages better; however, he tries to shrug off this instinct to disparage. He tries to assimilate, to take part, to be open-minded. Boy, does he try, but so far it's not working.

"You," says Björn to a woman near the front.

"Me?" she says.

"Yes, will you please come up and inspect the stage? Please walk around it and let everyone know what it's made out of."

The woman gets busy walking around the stage, stomping on it in places, doing a fine, thorough job. Then she says into Björn's mic, "The whole stage is carpeted and it feels like thin wood underneath it."

"And you are confident that the entire stage is carpeted with thin wood underneath it?"

She nods enthusiastically. "Absolutely, I'm confident of that."

"Thanks. You can go back to your seat. Let's give her a hand."

They give her a hand.

Then Björn pulls a wand out of thin air. He leans down at the feet of Sputtering Husband and Zombie Wife and taps several times on the carpeted stage. Now there's smoke wafting around their ankles, climbing up, encasing them in fog. Björn moves away and says, "Ladies and gentlemen, once the smoke clears, I think you'll find that my associates here are actually standing on *thin ice*."

The smoke clears and everyone struggles to see, jockeys

for a better view. Björn's associates are indeed standing on a small circle of thin ice. They shift from side to side, steadying their sneakers on the slick surface.

"Ooooh," everyone says in surprise.

"What the hell?" says somebody with a Scottish accent from the back.

"The rumors are true: Björn is a true sorcerer!" another guy shouts.

"Wow, it's sure hard to keep our lives stable standing on this *thin ice*," Zombie Wife says.

"The simplest task, such as just standing here, is a daunting endeavor," Sputtering Husband says. "I wonder what we can do to better our situation."

"Have any of you ever felt like this?" Björn asks the audience. There are thoughtful nods, murmurs in the affirmative, knowing and furtive glances between spouses. He continues his speech: "Remember, this couple up here is only one permutation of marital dynamics. Maybe you've never officially tied the knot but have lived together for many years. Maybe you're a same-sex couple. Maybe a long-distance relationship. Maybe your signs don't correspond to these up here in the slightest, but instead say things like PILL-POPPING FLOOZY, GAMBLES LIKE CRAZY, CLOSET CASE!, ADDICTED TO PORN, SHOPS FOR FULFILLMENT, VIOLENT STREAK, HUNG LIKE A TODDLER, DRUNK & INDIFFERENT, I'M SETTLING WITH YOU, BLOWS PAYCHECK AT TITTY BARS, YOU'RE THE WRONG ETHNICITY, COCAINE FOR BREAKFAST, DESIRES S&M BUT ASHAMED TO ADMIT IT, INFIDELITY EMPOWERS ME, I HATE OUR CHILDREN, TOO DAMAGED TO GIVE EMOTIONALLY, YOU EXACERBATE MY DADDY ISSUES, LOST IN SELF-PITY, HAVEN'T HEALED MY PAST TRAUMAS, etc., etc. In the long run, it makes no difference what your particular sign says. Point is that you are here to *recapture the magic*! Now, let me ask all of you a very serious question: How long can two people stand on *thin ice*?"

From the speakers comes the sound of cracking ice.

A few gasps from the audience . . .

"I'm feeling vulnerable to catastrophe," Zombie Wife says.

"I've come to expect the worst due to our pattern of toxic communication," Sputtering Husband muses.

The sounds of cracking, splintering ice grow louder.

And that's when Sputtering Husband and Zombie Wife fall through the ice and into water. They fall right into the stage and splash around. Holy smokes, Coffen can't believe his eyes. He didn't see a trapdoor on the stage earlier, let alone a patch of ice, let alone a patch of ice concealing a water tank. Wow! It's a magnificent trick—a feat of hearty magnitude.

"It's sure cold in here," Sputtering Husband says.

"If only we'd learned to *recapture the magic* prior to this disastrous yet inevitable conclusion," Zombie Wife says.

"Don't let this happen to you and yours," Björn says to the audience. "Trust me: We can fix whatever's ailing your relationships. I promise. Think of me as the Lifeguard of Love on Duty. If you fall into the frigid waters of marital discord, I can help you climb out before you freeze to death."

Coffen's internal clash to participate in this show hits a pothole as soon as the magician says "Lifeguard of Love." Bob almost laughs—it sounds too much like a porn: *Excuse me, scantily clad coed on the beach. Do you need CPR? My penis is really great at administering it.*

He stares at Jane, who still looks to be taking this all very seriously.

"Speaking of freezing to death," Sputtering Husband says through chattering teeth.

"In a minute," says Björn.

"My feet are numb," Zombie Wife says.

"Divas," Björn mutters, then helps both of them get out of the water. They stand onstage shivering and everyone gives a walloping round of applause before the two walk off and huddle in the corner in blankets.

"Do you know why they call me Björn the Bereft?" the magician asks. "Because of these." He points at his cheeks, which are slick with tears. "I've been crying nonstop for nine years. Nine! Ever since my own marriage failed. My wife and I weren't clearly reading each other's signs. Even if we don't wear real signs around our real necks in everyday life, they are invisibly dangling there. For instance, did I know that Vivian's invisible dangling sign said BORED IN THE BEDROOM? I had no idea of her boredom in the bedroom. How is anyone supposed to fix something if they aren't given ample opportunity to make adjustments? It's common sense, right? So tonight, you are going to articulate what your sign says to your spouse. Hopefully, this exercise can close some of the distance that exists between you. Will everyone please look under their placemats? What's there? Is there a blank dental bib that you can write on and then fasten around your neck? There sure is. And before you go giving me too much credit, no, that wasn't a magic trick. I had my interns stash those there before the show. I'm a magician of principles and won't take credit for feats I myself did not mastermind. You'll also notice a Sharpie next to your bread plate. Please take a couple minutes and collect your thoughts regarding what should be written on your dental bib. Remember: The sign is already invisibly dangling from your neck. Now, it's time to be honest with yourself, your partner, and do your best to make the marriage work. Trust me: You don't want to end up like me, crying for nine years. Could I have stopped crying by now? Yes and no. But I cast a spell on myself to cry every day for the rest of my life so I could help other people avoid the vipers' nest my wife and I stumbled into. Does that make me a martyr? Am I some kind of emotional hero? We'll see how history remembers my contribution to the dark arts. I can only hope to be immortalized in the pantheon of legendary illusionists."

Björn pauses, twirls the ends of his moustache. He's pacing back and forth in exaggerated, labored strides and making eye contact with all the people near the front, flashing them smiles. Probably the magician thinks he's being friendly, but all Bob sees is a snake oil salesman trying to dupe people into buying his miracle tonic.

Björn says, "Don't show your sign to your partner until I tell you to. For now, only worry about writing on it, then stand up next to your chair. Once everyone is standing, I'll know we're ready for the next phase. Good luck." He wipes more tears from his face.

Jane looks at Bob, but he can't read her expression. He wishes his wife were easier to decipher, like Dumper and his slithering tongue. No way to misinterpret that. But how's Coffen currently supposed to gauge Jane?

He smiles at her.

She immediately looks down at her dental bib.

They both prepare to write. Everyone in the place uses their forearms, hands, even elbows to block anybody from seeing their messages while they write, like kids in school trying to keep their test answers secret from nosy neighbors.

This is harder than it sounds; it seems to Bob that a task of this scale might take hours. Trying to distill the struggles in their lives down to one phrase. Trying to cook the writhing mess of human experience down to a single line. Coffen can't imagine how everyone here is supposed to diligently weigh the pros and cons, ponder the strengths and weaknesses and roots of the dissonances in their life as a couple, such a sprawling complex web of . . .

Then Jane rockets up.

She's the first person to stand, the first person to swiftly identify the problem.

It does not appear that she's seeing the strings that comprise the nuanced web of discord and instead easily zeroes in on what she deems their marriage's nemesis.

She holds her dental bib at her waist, facing it backward, so nobody can see it.

"That was fast," Coffen says to her.

"I know what I want to say."

"I can't think of anything."

"Go with your gut."

"One sec."

"You know what's wrong."

"I'm still thinking."

"Of course you are."

It sounds like a dig to Coffen: the way Jane says, *Of course you are*, like thinking is some kind of crime, like wanting to make an educated decision is a statement about Bob's inability to make decisions. Which of course isn't true. Not just anybody would have heaved the patriotic javelin toward the window; they'd have settled on hitting the flowerpot, now wouldn't they? Bob faced down a bully and was born anew. That night, Bob felt himself reboot, felt himself start over. No longer was he going to be some kind of human punching bag. Hell no. And tonight is the chance for him to do the same thing with his marriage. Tonight is a way for them to refresh themselves, install updates. Tonight is a system wipe.

Everyone is standing and waiting for him to finish writing.

Jane looms, bouncing one of her legs in a quick rhythm. Coffen can see her anger. It's in the eyes. Yikes, it's even in the nose and eyebrows and wrinkles. It's in the way she stares and shakes her head back and forth.

"Almost done," Bob says.

"Jesus, just pick something!" Jane says.

"I'm trying."

"This is what's wrong with our marriage. Do something, Bob. Act. Be here!"

Coffen can see her frustration cranking to ire. She thinks he's floundering, though that's not what he's doing, at least not intentionally. He's being thorough, practical, shrewd. Then it dawns on Bob that the night with Schumann is the key for how best to convey his newfound message—people will keep ramming you into the oleanders forever if you let them. You have to be your own defender.

Coffen hurriedly writes his message.

Then he joins his standing comrades.

He smiles at Jane, who averts her eyes to the stage, keeps shaking her head.

"One last word to the wise," says Björn. "Seeing your partner's sign is not going to be easy. It might make you mad or sad or defensive. These are all valid responses. Maybe you can go so far as to say they're inevitable. But remember that tonight is merely Step 1 of the process. And what's

Step 1? Step 1 is 'Read the Signs.' Step 2 is my intermediate show, which I highly recommend. For tonight, you are honestly sharing your vulnerabilities with each other, and maybe it's been several years since you've been honest in the relationship. Otherwise, why would you be here? So no matter how hard it is to read your partner's sign, try and put your own self aside and see what has caused your partner to feel the way they currently feel.

"In retrospect, I think Vivian was bored in the bedroom because I have a low testosterone count. That's not my fault, people, that's science. However, if Vivian had been willing to turn her invisible dangling sign into a visible dangling sign and communicate her heart's true feelings, I could have gone to the doctor and gotten a shot and my testosterone could have exploded through the roof. Do you see what I mean? So read the signs, no matter how painful the message might be: I'm offering a chance to save your marriage. Now make sure that you and your spouse position yourselves on the red X taped on the floor behind your seats. Stand less than a foot apart from each other and directly on the X. Here goes . . ."

The lights go dark again.

The prerecorded heartbeat thumps from the speakers.

Everybody attaches their dental bibs.

Björn the Bereft says, "Abracadabra . . . Abracadabra . . . Abracadabra!"

Everything becomes clear as the room is lit once more.

▪ Thin ice ▪

Here's what comes clear as the room is lit once more: First, Bob and Jane are no longer standing on the red X on the carpeted floor. They, like Sputtering Husband and Zombie Wife, are now standing on *thin ice*. Bob Coffen taps his foot on it, leans down to touch it, verifying that this isn't some kind of optical illusion. It is not. Coffen looks around at the other couples whose feet he can see, and they, too, are all perfectly framed in their own small circles of ice.

A slap!

A woman slugs a man whose sign says ASIAN FETISH and WIFE'S NOT ASIAN. He falls flat on his ass on the ice. It shatters and both husband and wife crash through it, flailing around helplessly in the freezing water, panting for air.

Another couple bickers close by the Coffens. The guy says, "So that's how you really feel?" and she says, "Yeah, that's how I feel all right," and he says, "I knew you didn't forgive me," and she says, "You don't deserve forgiveness," and the bottom falls out and down they fall through the ice.

Other couples crash through their small frozen ponds, too. Ice explodes all around. These couples are in the midst of arguments, spats, screaming matches that Coffen can't quite hear, but it's easy to transcribe the sentiments: They are embarrassed and brokenhearted and enraged at what's written on their partners' dental bibs, and they can't control their ire, can't see that there might be truth written on the dangling signs: All they see are profane accusations.

More ice smashes.

More couples coughing and wading in the water.

Coffen sees one couple holding their ground nicely. They are nodding, hugging, kissing. Their ice appears stable.

It's all such an overwhelming scene that Coffen hasn't yet read Jane's sign, but now his eyes move toward her dental bib. He's so scared. Petrified that her sign will say SUCKING GOTTHORM COMPLETES ME. Or: NOBODY PILLAGES LIKE GOTTHORM! Or worse yet: I'M IN LOVE WITH GOTTHORM. Or it might not have anything to do with her water-treading coach. She might not be having an affair at all. Coffen is in no direct way suspicious of infidelity, but he frankly can't believe that Jane is satisfied with their sex life. A woman has certain needs, after all. So does her husband, if anybody's asking.

His eyes finally find her sign and here's what it says: NEEDS REASON TO KEEP TRYING.

Immediately, Coffen's psyche starts thrashing—instantaneously the severity of this evening slams into him like a drunk driver. Jane, his steady Jane, his practically minded Jane—she took time off her training schedule to come here tonight. Under normal circumstances, Jane would mock this. Mock Schumann's bagpipes. Roll her eyes at Björn. She'd call the members of his audience livestock searching for the easiest answers money can buy. But that's not what she did at all. In fact, she insisted that the Coffens come. It's dawning on Bob that NEEDS REASON TO KEEP TRYING isn't an early warning. It's a final notice. It's a death rattle.

The other thing that concerns Bob is reading Jane's sign identifies a weakness in his own. Jane's bib documents something that has to do with them both, their relationship, and Coffen thought only of himself on his sign, which says SMEARED IN THE OLEANDERS.

Jane's eyes train on Bob's bib. She tilts her head at it, looking perplexed, probably trying to work out its meaning.

Coffen hears their *thin ice* cracking.

"Are you making fun of this?" Jane asks.

"Let's talk about it later, sweetie," Bob says, worrying about falling through the ice.

"Are you making fun of me?"

"Let's kiss and hug now and then we can really talk about it all later when we get home."

"There is no guarantee of later," she says. "That's why we're here."

The volume of ice cracking gets louder.

"Shhhh," Bob says to her.

"Do you know how hard it was for me to be honest?"

"Shhhh. Stop arguing with me or we'll fall."

"You mock all this right to my fucking face?"

"Let me explain what I mean by my sign."

"If you have to explain your sign, then it's a shitty sign."

"I think we're going in the drink," Coffen says, solely focused on the *thin ice*.

"Forget it," she says. She pulls off her dental bib, sets it on the table. "I need to be away from you right now."

"The oleanders are from the other night with Schumann. Let me tell you the whole story of what happened there."

"No more stories."

"Jane, I'm a little lost right now, okay? I'm turned around. I don't know who I am. I want to know who I am again."

"You're Bob," she says, turning to leave.

"Yes, Bob is me."

"You have a wife and two kids. You shouldn't work so many hours. You're compulsively online. And you're acting like a total asshole tonight."

With that, the ice buckles, but Jane has already moved off of their small circle, walking toward the ballroom's exit. Coffen falls through the ice and into the water. He splashes around all by himself.

"I am Bob! Bob is me!" he calls to her, choking, treading water. "I want to try!" He gasps for air. Coughs. "There are reasons to keep trying!"

But she doesn't stop. Coffen watches her leave and thinks of Schumann's taillights moving away, the night he was smeared in the oleanders.

▪ Seriously going loco ▪

Interns with poles help the fallen couples out of the icy water. Not every couple falls, and those who are still nice and dry now hug ravenously. This experience has bonded them in a way that makes all the wet/no-bonders despise these public shows of affection.

Coffen treads water until an acned intern helps him get out of the cold water.

"Where's your wife, bro?"

"She left."

"That sucks."

Bob runs out of the ballroom. He is dripping wet. He is running and he is dripping wet and he is yelling, "Jane! Jane! We have reasons to keep trying! Honest! We have good reasons to keep it up! I want to try!"

He runs past the hotel's restaurant, past a sports bar adjacent to the lobby. He asks the concierge if he's seen Jane, gives him a description of her, emphasizing the braids.

"Would you like a towel, sir?"

"I'd like my wife."

"Right, of course. No doubt. But in the meantime, what do you think of drying off with a towel?"

Bob sees public restrooms on the other side of the lobby, sprints over and holds the door open to the ladies' room, and says, "Jane! Let's talk it out! I'm ready to try if you're ready to try!"

"Get out of here, you Peeping Tom," a lady's voice says.

"Is there anyone else in here who happens to be named Jane?" Bob asks.

Nothing for a few seconds.

"I'm texting my nephew who's a cop," the lady says.

Coffen goes sprinting outside, sees the SUV.

"So?" Schumann says, waiting in the hotel's side lot, holding his bagpipes, maybe practicing before Bob got there. "How did it go?"

"Where's Jane?"

"I haven't seen her."

"I've looked everywhere and can't track her down," says Coffen.

"Why are you all wet?"

"The magician sabotaged some of us. He threw us in an ice bath. I lost Jane in the melee."

"Sounds like a cool show."

Bob opens the SUV's passenger door. "It was not a cool show at all."

Schumann shuts the door. "Don't climb in my car."

"Why not?"

"My seats are leather and you're soaked. You need to dry off properly before getting in."

"There's no time."

"There's still time on the game clock."

"We have to find Jane."

"Dry off. You can use my gym towel in the back. I'll get it."

"Schumann, I'm ordering you to drive!" Bob says.

But Schumann's not having it: "Listen, your life coach

got leather seats last week and won't have them ruined. Come on, I'm playing along, doing my part. Do you think this is easy for me to take orders from you? It's not. I've been a QB since elementary school."

Schumann hands Coffen the towel. "I'm playing out of position. Psycho Schumann is supposed to be the star. You can't expect me to get it right away. I'm used to the limelight."

"We have to get to my house right now. I need to talk to Jane."

"I know a shortcut," says Schumann, making a face like he's scrutinizing Coffen's technique with the towel.

■ ■ ■

Schumann speeds around the hotel's back lot, and that's when Coffen spies Björn the Bereft, loading some boxes into his trunk.

"It's him," says Bob.

"The magician?"

"The marriage ruiner."

Schumann stops the SUV. "This is your opponent, huh?"

"Forget it," Coffen says. "He sucks, but we need to get to Jane."

"Not so fast."

"We have to hurry."

"This guy shall pay for throwing you into the ice bath."

"Come on, let's go," Bob says, getting a bad feeling about the deranged look in Schumann's eyes.

"As your life coach, I need to share an idea with you," says Schumann. "You may not like it at first, but let it marinate before answering me."

"What?"

"We need that magician to accompany us to your house."

"What are you talking about?"

"For Jane," Schumann says. "Jane wanted to go to the show tonight, right? You told me this was her idea. She respects that magician. You said so yourself that he's the marriage ruiner. He needs to make it right. Jane needs to hear it straight from the horse's mouth."

"He won't help us."

"He might help us against his will."

"Let's take off."

"We could throw him in the back of the SUV and see what happens."

"I don't think so."

"We could demand his presence on a trip to your house."

"Kidnap him?"

"Kidnapping is a word streaked with evil," Schumann says.

Coffen can't believe his ears, can barely compute what's coming out of Schumann's mouth. It's so ludicrous that Bob just isn't taking the quarterback's threats seriously—how can he? How can he ponder anything except getting to Jane and telling her the truth? He's lost and he knows he's lost and he wants to do something about it, wants to crawl out of his stupor and be a better man.

"You want to abduct a magician?"

Schumann breaks into a batch of slow, awestruck applause. "Do I have the look of someone seriously going loco, Coffen? Are you seeing my game face? Are you scared of the warrior thriving in my guts?"

"Please, Schumann, let's just go."

"You want me to help you hijack this jag-off, don't you? Is that what you're saying?"

"That's exactly what I'm not saying."

"You want me to be the muscle of the operation? I say abso-fucking-lutely. I say let's get loco. I haven't done anything crazy since leaving Purdue. We used to leave a path of destruction in our wake." Schumann's voice is getting really loud: "And now, I shall quarterback a vessel of mayhem once more!"

He starts whistling the beginning bars of "Hail Purdue" to properly motivate himself.

"I'll be right back," he says to Coffen, who's trying to formulate words, any words, but he sits there stupidly as Schumann exits the SUV. It's like Bob's witnessing somebody else's hallucination—so surreal that all he can do is whisper, "Don't, please," but Schumann's already outside the vehicle.

Schumann rolls his sleeves up to his elbows.

He ambles toward the magician, who's still standing at his trunk, and asks him, "Have you ever seen a fourth-quarter comeback in which the underdog snatches victory from the rabid jaws of defeat?"

"What are you talking about?" Björn asks, wiping some tears from his cheeks.

■ Dip his haunches in honey mustard ■

All Bob Coffen can think is this: *Life coaches are not supposed to kidnap magicians.* It must be some kind of unwritten life-coach rule—do not creep up and head-butt the magician. Do not give him the fireman carry and toss him in the backseat of your SUV.

Psycho Schumann's not interested in any industry standards; he makes up his own rules as the night goes on. While they drive away, Coffen's eyeballs Ping-Pong between Schumann and Björn, who's starting to come to.

"I see you're taking a very literal interpretation of capturing the magic," Björn says in the SUV, mindlessly scratching at his moustache. "It's a metaphor, you retards."

"Is that any way to ingratiate yourself to your captors?" says Schumann. "You come into our stadium and start calling us retarded?"

"What stadium?" Björn says.

"We have to let him out of the car," Bob says.

"We'll all get out together at your house," Schumann says.

"Schumann, let's be reasonable," Bob says.

"I'd drink the blood of a Notre Dame lineman right now," Schumann says.

"I will put a curse something fierce on your asses if you don't let me out right now," says Björn.

Bob giggles and says, "A curse? Really?"

"I'd dip that lineman's haunches in honey mustard and gorge like a king."

"You saw what I did in the ballroom," Björn says to Bob. "I'm assuming your soaked bib and wet head means you went in the water tank. Sorry about that. But what you're doing right now, you're going to regret forever."

"This isn't my idea," Coffen says. "He's acting on his own accord."

"Tell that to the police," Björn says.

"I feel totally alive again, Coffen," Schumann says. "Our kidnapping has awoken the sleeping gladiator in me. All I see around me are football games."

"I'm talking the kind of curse that ancient civilizations wrote about," Björn says. "You two retards will be immortalized in an allegory about what happens when you tempt fate and have to suffer the dire consequences of the dark arts."

"If it were up to me, I'd let you go right now," Coffen says.

"You're on the hook for this, too. Are you sure you want to mess with me?" Björn says.

"He doesn't listen to me," Coffen says, pointing at Schumann.

"Try harder to convince him."

"He wants to take you to my house, so you can help me and my wife. I think she's going to divorce me."

"I've been there. You heard my story from the show. But think, man: You're going to get arrested," Björn says. "You'll go to prison. But if you let me out now, I won't call the cops or anything. Honest. I promise. A magician's word is a two-ton brick of gold."

"Hike the ball!" Schumann yells in the driver's seat.

"Hike the ball and let the fur fly! Let's scrap like junkyard dogs!"

"Think about it," Björn says. "You're doing this for your wife? Do you have children, too?"

"Yes."

"Well, what good will you do them once you're in the clink?"

Reflexively, Bob begins to answer—begins a fumbling phrase, a polluted cluster of nonsense—because the truth is he can't defend himself, or Schumann, or any of this. It's wrong. He's wrong. And even if this whole ordeal is Schumann's idea, won't the police assume Coffen is guilty by association?

Bob feels a throb in his guts and barely rolls the SUV's window down in time before he throws up everywhere.

"Don't worry about that," says Schumann. "I tossed my cookies before we went for the state title in high school. Nerves are good. They mean you're starving for victory. But if the puke damages my paint job, you're footing the bill."

"Stop the SUV," Coffen says to Schumann.

"Why?"

"Stop it."

"I can't do that."

"Pull over."

"We're driving the ball. We're almost to the end zone. Soon we'll celebrate victory with dances of ecstasy. Back flips. Ceremonial chants. Cheerleaders flipping their tiny skirts up."

"We have to let him go," Bob says.

"We're almost the champions," Schumann says.

"The champions of what?" Björn says.

"The kidnapping champions."

"Stop the SUV!" shouts Bob.

"No," Schumann says. "I'm calling an audible."

"What's that even mean?" Coffen says.

"It means I've come to the line of scrimmage. I've looked over the defensive formation. And at the last second, I'm changing the play. You're telling me the play is to pull over and let this magician go scot-free. And I'm telling you that I won't run that play. I'm calling something different."

Coffen says, "Listen to me, Schumann. This isn't a game. This is real. We are committing a crime. We will get arrested. Snap out of it."

"Feels too good to be competing in a game again."

It's that mention of the word "game"—Coffen and Schumann have totally different definitions of gaming. Bob controls his avatar. Bob competes in a controlled environment. Yet for Schumann, the stakes are real. His adrenaline is like gasoline and Bob thinks that he has to appeal to Schumann's sense of family: The only way Schumann will come to his senses, snap out of this trance, is if he's going to lose much more than a game, much more than blowing out a knee, his career over—he's going to lose his status quo. His wife. His child. And hopefully, he won't squander all that for an orgasm of endorphins.

"Think of going to jail and never kissing your wife again," Bob says.

"I'm a tiger breaking out of my cage with a laser cannon and a top-shelf vendetta."

"Think of never spooning her."

"I'm a king cobra poised to strike and my fangs have been coated in a tincture of nuclear waste and hot lava."

Okay, so his missus isn't the pressure point that Coffen needs to push. How can he get this game's character to do what he wants? Last ditch effort: "Think of little Schu. Can you imagine little Schu without you?"

Suddenly, Schumann's whole face changes. Trance shattered. His eyes fill with tears, though he's able to choke them back.

"Little Schu?" Schumann says, almost in a whisper.

"Don't deprive him of your loving guidance."

"I never really had a father," Schumann says.

"Me neither," Coffen says.

"Neither did I," says Björn from the backseat. "America is full of deadbeat dads. They're like crabs in our country's pubes."

"Little Schu deserves a papa," Schumann says, pulling the car over.

"I'm sorry," Coffen says to the magician. "Please don't call the cops."

"I went a little crazy when my wife left me, too," Björn says.

"Little Schu needs to know all my tricks of the trade. I have to pass on my secrets. Every rookie needs a cagey veteran to show him the ropes."

Björn gets out of the SUV and says to Bob, "Look, I'm trying to be understanding. You fell through the ice. You're obviously having some kind of psychotic break induced by your wheezing marriage. Like I said, I went off the rails when my wife left me. But do me a favor and try to make this the dumbest thing you ever do. And appreciate my incredible empathy. Most men would not be cool about this. The world already has plenty of psychotics. Get your shit together."

"I don't think I'm psychotic," Coffen says.

"Would you consider yourself more of a recreational kidnapper?" Björn asks.

"Okay, okay," Bob says. "You're not seeing me at my best. But thank you for your mercy."

"I'm going to teach little Schu to throw a spiral tonight," Schumann says.

Björn says to Coffen while he points at Schumann, "You shouldn't spend time with that guy. I can tell you have at least one redeeming quality, maybe two. But that guy's off his rocker."

"Off my pigskin rocker."

"Here's one last trick," Björn says, "to show I have a heart and won't kick a man who's in the middle of a midlife crisis. Look in your jacket pocket."

Coffen does as he's told, and there are two tickets to Björn's intermediate show on Sunday evening: the night Step 2 is laid out for all in attendance.

"How did you do that?" Bob asks.

"I'll never tell."

"Why would you help me after what we did?"

"Please, I did something much worse than you when my wife left me." Björn shakes his head. "It's all so fragile, right? I mean, we're all so fragile."

The magician walks away from the SUV and Coffen thinks: *We are brittle beings, easily breakable, buried under circumstances.* Maybe these circumstances snow down in flurries, except the flakes are made of fluorescent orange, the bright color pocking Bob's skin so everyone knows how lost he is. He staggers the streets slathered in the stuff, a fluorescent orange monster making things worse.

▪ Cops and monsters ▪

It had been a silent ride home, post-Björn. Coffen couldn't find any words to talk about how disappointed he was in himself so he stewed in self-disgust, every now and again basting every bit of his psyche in the juice of Jane walking out of the ballroom, leaving him alone on their *thin ice*. Schumann couldn't do much of anything except drive well under the posted speed limit and periodically peep to himself, "Little Schu . . . little Schu . . . little Schu . . ."

Now, he drops Coffen off at home, and Bob's scourge of a mother-in-law is out on the front steps, waiting for him with her wicked, diabetic smile. She drums her fingers on her knee.

Erma says to Bob, "It's my esteemed honor to alert you that you are not welcome here until after Jane goes for the world record. And, maybe, you might not be welcomed back then, either."

"Wait, what?"

"For now, assume you can come back after her record attempt. Probably."

"That's not until Monday."

"What's that thing around your neck?"

"It's a dental bib."

"Why?"

"Long story."

"We think it's best for Jane if she's not burdened with the sights or sounds of you."

"Who's 'we'?"

"Me, Jane, and Gotthorm."

"You, Jane, and Gotthorm."

"Yes, we're concerned that your being is like an anchor around her neck. You pull her to the bottom of the pool."

"I'm not an anchor."

"Agree to disagree, Bob."

"Can I please talk to her? I'll leave right after, but I need to talk to her, explain what happened back there at the magic show."

"She made it crystal clear that speaking with you is the last itty-bitty thing on earth she wants to do."

"Where am I supposed to go?"

"Motels are lovely this time of year," says Erma. "Entire guidebooks are devoted to their panoramic beauty."

"Can I get some things first?"

She hands Coffen a plastic bag with his toothbrush, no toothpaste, nothing else at all.

"What about clothes?" he whines. "I'm still wet."

"I'll bring a suitcase by your office on Monday, before she goes for the record."

"It's Friday night. What am I supposed to wear?"

"Don't raise your voice with me."

"Can I at least see the kids?"

"Of course. They're obviously asleep now, but you can see them this weekend. Call me first. We think notice is important. We are advocates of respected boundaries."

"Listen, I know you don't unconditionally love me," says Bob.

"We do not love you."

"But I'm the father of your grandchildren."

"Uh-huh," Erma says, a look on her face like Bob's asking for directions to a destination that she feels like keeping secret.

"Yeah, I'm scared she might make me permanently move out of our house."

"Uh-huh," she says.

Coffen knows he's not going to win, says, "Can you grab one other thing for me from inside the house?"

"You're sure pushing your luck right now."

"Sorry, I need it for work. It's sitting in the downstairs hallway. It's a kind of clock with an engraving on it."

"I saw that."

"Can you grab it for me? I need it for this project I'm working on."

"Fine," she says, going in and coming back out of the house in under twenty seconds. She hands the plock to him and says, "We appreciate you stopping by."

Coffen puts the plastic bag with his toothbrush in his pocket, clutches the plock, and walks toward his car. Driving with his hurt shoulder isn't ideal, but it's better than dealing with Schumann right now—his athletically inspired help would only make Bob feel worse, as would his quiet woeful murmurings, "Little Schu . . . little Schu . . ."

Besides, Bob needs to talk to somebody who will listen to him and Schumann doesn't fit that description. Who does in Bob's life? Jane is the only person he's confided in since they've been married. He has old friends, sure, but nobody he feels comfortable calling up out of the blue. He's on his own, he guesses. On his own to figure out how to clean all this fluorescent orange off him.

■ ■ ■

Bob's first stop is Taco Shed. It's after midnight and he's never been here so late, though this is his favorite fast food, a lunchtime staple. He turns into the drive-through, only one car in front of him up at the intercom.

A couple storefronts down in the strip mall, he sees two people polishing a statue of the Buddha out front of a temple that used to be a SportsZone. Why they're doing this task so late, he'll never know, but give them credit: Even at this time of night, the shine they're whipping up on the deity is impressive.

Waiting patiently . . .

But two minutes becomes three . . .

Becomes five.

And five minutes waiting behind one vehicle in a Taco Shed drive-through is unheard of, especially because Bob is steeped in this particular drive-through's traffic patterns as only a top-notch connoisseur can be. His enthusiasm for Mexican lasagnas makes Coffen conspicuous around Taco Shed—he sometimes goes there more than once a day. He gets self-conscious when he doubles-up his greasy treks, which makes him bashful around the employees, assuming that once he motors off they all gossip about the sad man with a tapeworm that can only be sated on a steady diet of Mexican lasagnas.

He toots the horn, which gets a whole heap of nothing as a response. He rolls down his window and says, "What are you doing up there?"

Another horn toot produces zilch, and Coffen sees nary another option but to do some reconnaissance work.

Throw the car in park.

Wing open the door.

Approach the inexplicably idling vehicle.

Coffen sees a guy in the driver's seat passed out cold, sleeping with a whiskey bottle wedged in his crotch and $20 bills scattered about. What he hears, however, is a woman's scratchy voice coming from the drive-through intercom, saying, "Well, Otis, I got my panties down at my ankles and I'm ready to be mounted. Mount me, Otis! Mount me something fierce!"

Safe to say this stops Coffen dead in his famished tracks.

More from the scratchy raw lady voice coming sexily from the intercom: "Otis, I like my men to yank my hair a bit when they come up from behind. You gonna yank my hair and drive me crazy, Otis, you old goat?"

Bob shakes Otis, who isn't big on answering or moving, but is sleeping soundly with some spittle dripping from his mouth. Shakes him once more for good measure and the scratchy raw lady voice says, "Otis, I'm waiting for your hard taco meat to slide in my wet taco shell!"

"Hello?" Coffen says to her.

"Who the hell's that?" says the lady without much friskiness behind these words.

"A paying customer who's hungry."

Then the voice pauses, makes some phony computer beeping noises, and finally says in a robot voice, "We are experiencing some technical difficulties with this intercom system. For example, unofficial messages totally unaffiliated with this fine establishment have been mysteriously beamed here from places unknown, maybe outer space, and please keep in mind that the words currently reaching your eardrums from this malfunctioning intercom system have not been approved by any sanctioning body. We hope to have this situation remedied quickly and are so sorry for the inconvenience."

More phony computer beeping noises.

"You're not fooling anybody," Coffen says.

A dramatic exhale from her and then, "Otis, you know the rules. You can't bring any friends along."

"Pardon me," Coffen says to her. "I can't order because this drunk is asleep in his car."

The scratchy lady voice sighs. "Not again."

"Not again?"

"Hold up a minute," she says.

Coffen looks at Otis, poor guy grabbing some shut-eye at the drive-through intercom. Life could be worse, right? At least Bob doesn't binge-drink and go dead to the world getting intercom hanky-panky at Taco Shed.

He says to Otis, "Looks like you're going to have to jerk it the old-fashioned way tonight, my friend."

Still nothing from the narcotized Casanova.

Then the back door opens and a woman with gargantuan muscles spilling from her official uniform storms out. Her nametag says Tilda. Coffen has seen this woman many times before and is always impressed with her many muscles, like a bodybuilder. She's probably fifty years old and too tanned and Coffen feels thankful not to be Otis yanking Tilda's hair and mounting her from behind.

"Hey, I know you," says Tilda.

Coffen actually blushes. Jane is doing her best to break the world's treading-water record and Bob is poised to be the first human to munch one million Mexican lasagnas. "I know you too."

"You're here all the time."

"Not all the time."

"Yeah, you're the *capitán* of Mexican lasagnas," she says with a Spanish flare.

If it's possible, Bob blushes even more. "I guess I am."

"*Capitán*, I'd like to apologize," Tilda says, "for this strange man that I've never seen before sitting in his car, obviously inebriated. This is an injustice and on behalf of Taco Shed, I'd like to prepare you a complimentary gourmet meal." She puts a muscled paw through Otis's window and gives him a spank on the face, very hard, and Otis stirs awake and stretches with surprise. "Get out of here, you strange stranger," Tilda says. "Get out of here before I alert the proper authorities to your inebriated state of mind. You are a public nuisance, and I'm aghast by this strange stranger's actions!"

A groggy Otis is confused but understands enough to make a quick run for it, moving the sloshing whiskey to the passenger seat and driving off.

"What do you mean you don't know him?" Coffen asks her. "You called him by name."

"You a cop?"

"Do I look like a cop?"

"These days, everyone looks like a cop, and that's why it's getting so hard to break the law—used to be the police were all white guys with crew cuts and cheap shoes. You could spot 'em a mile away, but these days, wow, I'm going to need to see some ID."

"You want to see ID that says I'm not a cop?"

"Yeah."

"Do they make those?"

"They sure as shit should," says Tilda. Then she seems to lose her drooping gall. "I can't keep up the charade any longer. You got me, cop. I'll sign my confession. I'll waive my right to a speedy trial. The men have to say a secret phrase into the intercom. They have to say, 'Hark the herald angel likes to watch TV in his birthday suit.' See what I mean? No one else would come up to the intercom and say that accidentally, so I thought I'd make a little extra dough on the sly and no one would ever know, but this drunken perv is always passing out on me at the intercom and now a damn cop happens to stumble upon our impure exchange."

"Will you relax and make me something to eat? I'm not a police officer. I build video games." Coffen thinks that maybe humor might set her mind at ease. "The *capitán* of Mexican lasagnas is no friend of the *policía*."

"Typical cop behavior."

"I'm really hungry."

"This smacks of entrapment."

"Your paranoia has paranoia," Coffen says.

"You gum as much blotter acid as I did, and you live the rest of your life convinced everyone's a cop."

"I only want a Mexican lasagna."

Tilda eyeballs Bob, probably searching for some sort of tell to indicate whether he's a cop or not, but realizing there's no way to know for certain. She says, "How about three Mexican lasagnas?"

"Deal." Coffen nods and she says she'll go inside, prep the grub. He walks back to his car and pulls it up to the intercom and says, "And also a Coke, please."

"The beverage will be complimentary as well on account of Taco Shed appreciating your patience with our malfunctioning intercom," Tilda says through the not-malfunctioning intercom. "I'll deliver them personally to you out back, once it's all ready."

Soon, this strange woman opens the back door again

and brings the booty of Mexican lasagnas, then hands Coffen his drink. She has one Mexican lasagna for herself, too. It's a tortilla filled with refried beans, marinara sauce, and processed cheese. They both get busy chowing down.

"This can't be a coincidence," Bob says.

"What?"

"On my way here, I was thinking that I needed somebody to talk to, and you're like a therapist."

"I don't think so."

"But sort of."

"Sorry to burst your bubble, but therapists aren't helping their clients pull their pud."

Coffen nods, takes another bite of Mexican lasagna. "Your secret is safe with me."

"Thanks. You don't even want to know how bad I need the money. You don't wanna hear about my daughter living in her boyfriend's car, and that's only the tip of the iceberg. Ain't these weird times? Lately, life's like one gigantic cartoon, and all I see are cops and monsters."

"I've been thinking that life is pretty much a no-win situation," he says, done with his first Mexican lasagna and sipping from the Coke.

"How's that?"

"I seem to be in the process of ruining everything."

"Are you going to knock it off? The ruining, I mean."

"I'm trying."

"Men love to say that they're trying. But really, you either do something or you don't. Trying is for babies learning to walk."

In principle, Coffen agrees with what Tilda is saying—*trying* is the most tired excuse out there. The worst part is that it's not even true, in Coffen's case. He's not trying. If he had been trying, Jane wouldn't have had to stoop to a magician for marital help.

"I miss babies," says Bob. "I loved napping with my daughter asleep on my chest."

"How old are yours?"

"Twelve and nine."

"Those ages are still fun," Tilda says. "Wait until they shack up in Roy's car with a bun in the oven and a meth habit. Then we'll talk."

Bob loves Tilda's honesty. When do you cross paths with somebody who so freely talks about their family's dirty laundry? First, the intercom-sex scam and now her daughter squatting in Roy's car. Her honesty makes Bob feel that he can confide, too. He says, "My kids aren't the problem. I'm the problem."

"Wait until you hand your daughter a notice for jury duty through Roy's car window."

"I'm glad to hear it gets worse."

"Everything gets worse," Tilda says. "It's one of the perks of being alive."

"Do you really believe that?"

"More often than not."

"Thanks for the free food," Coffen says. "And for talking to me. I needed to talk and you're wrong, you are a sort of therapist. Truth is, I'm lost."

"You're trying and you're lost. That's not a winning combination."

"I just need one thing to go right in my life."

"How's this? I'm giving you a free lifetime supply of Mexican lasagna," she says, "and if you're a perv, you can have a trial-subscription to my intercom-sex operation."

Beggars can't be choosers, Bob thinks. Beggars also can't

get enough Mexican lasagna, so this is really working out in Coffen's pathetic favor.

"Do you remember the magic words I told you?" Tilda asks.

"Yeah."

"I'm alone here from ten to three most nights. Any time in that window is fine, just say the magic words and drop your trousers."

"Can I talk to you about non-dirty stuff? Can I come by and chat?"

"My gifts of gab are of the more pervy variety. But I can make an exception for someone who's trying and lost."

"Thanks."

"And it's not all bad," Tilda says. "There's still fun in life."

"Oh yeah?"

"You've got to look real close."

"Look where?"

"Between the cops and monsters," she says.

▪ Rum: the other white meat ▪

Bob hopes that a coding bender might take his mind off the fact he's bedding down at Dumper Games tonight. It's past 3:00 AM, though the plock, which sits on his desk, reads midnight. Regardless of the time, sleep feels impossible, so he's up and at his computer, laying the framework for Scroo Dat Pooch. Of course, he'd rather be building anything else, but even this schlock is a distraction, busywork for his brain, a way to shove aside what happened earlier with Jane and Björn. Yes, even the asinine premise of Scroo Dat Pooch allows Bob to find escape from the shame of how he acted.

That's how it's always worked for Bob. There's always been escape while he coded. It's like alcohol or pills or whatever vice somebody else uses to block away things about their own lives they can't deal with. Bob uses computer code. Bob uses games. He uses his characters, the art of constructing entire worlds. He finds a swaddling delight in the fact he can use his imagination to create another reality, no matter how other aspects of his personal reality seem to tell him how he flounders or spoils things: how he's so painfully average; how he often feels unfit for the simplest tasks.

For example, other human beings seem to find pleasure

in getting up and going to work—others seem to be able to abide by the five days a week of an insipid job that does nothing except automatically deposit funds in a checking account; others have let the selfish, artistic dreams from their twenties crumble and slough, embracing the realities of life in their late thirties. But not Bob: His coding used to offer him pure time-stopping happiness, and now nothing feels pure. Nothing is naked. Everything is spurred by duty. There's private school to fund from kindergarten through senior year. There's a mortgage. There's the tyrannical arm of the HOA, which loves to spend the money of those entrenched in the subdivision. Car insurance alone is over $1,800 a month for the Coffens. There are college tuitions to grow. There's retirement. There's an urn.

Yes, Bob has fallen into the most predictable trap that exists in middle age: He's devolved into a function. He does the stuff he has to do. He buys the stuff he has to purchase. He goes places to keep the peace, waddles down the path of least resistance. He's devoid of identity. He's a thing.

And he resents himself for walking into this booby trap. Resents that it's his fault. It was his responsibility to build a life for himself that kept valuing his art. It was his, not Jane's, not the kids. It was nobody else's duty to make sure Coffen kept building games that sated his creative streak. He had to be in charge of carving the time to stay an artist, not a for-hire hack who builds games about bestiality. It was up to Bob to take care of Bob, just like everyone else on the planet has to take care of themselves. So why was this so hard for him? Why couldn't Coffen set aside a few nights a week to do what used to bring him so much pleasure, so much identity? The late nights were there, though he spent his free time killing time, drinking vodka and surfing the Internet for the pristine nether regions of unabashed coeds.

It isn't lost on Coffen that the thing he loves doing most, building nuanced worlds in his games, is the one thing he can't do in his own life. And if he can do it, he has no idea how to get started. Games always come with menus, instructions that explain how to play them, how to navigate and thrive in this environment, how to work toward winning. So what's the real-world equivalent of that? What's out there to teach Coffen?

■ ■ ■

Bob wakes up on a beanbag in the conference room. It's Saturday morning, and being at the office is in no way restoring Coffen's self-esteem. Not that there's much that he should feel good about anyway. At least he made some headway on Scroo Dat Pooch. At least by fixating on the game he found a way to ignore the horrid levels of shame slamming in his psyche.

Today, however, before his groggy mind goes back to work, his nose alerts him to a delectable presence in his proximity.

French toast.

Coffen trails it to the kitchen and sees one of the building's janitors, Ace, standing at the stove, a bottle of rum sitting on the countertop. Coffen often sees Ace around the office, but they never converse, save for the occasional tragic workplace platitude—*Man, do I got a case of the Mondays! I'm jonesing for a siesta! Friday can't come fast enough, huh?*

Ace isn't clad in his official janitor garb—in fact, he's

not clad in much at all, wearing an open bathrobe showing yellow boxer shorts. It makes Coffen think of Gotthorm, if Gotthorm decided to let himself go. Wow, does Bob wish Gotthorm would let himself go . . .

"Jesus, you scared me," Ace says.

Protocol might dictate a bathrobe-cinch once he sees Coffen enter the galley, but it appears that Ace isn't one for standard operating procedures.

"You sleeping here, too?" Ace asks.

Coffen pauses at this, ponders office rumors, premature stories of divorce, rueful glances from coworkers half his age, chomping for his job. Show no weakness! "Nope. Putting in some extra hours."

Ace smiles. "Then neither am I. And I definitely didn't take a bath in one of the tubs in LapLand. That's for sure."

LapLand is one of the unusual accoutrements that DG offers its employees. It's a room that has two endless pools—ten-foot tubs in which employees can swim against a manufactured current, covering great distances without ever moving from one freestyling or backstroking spot. Not only are these pools available for any employee to enjoy, but safety is key: There's a lifeguard on duty, should anybody cramp up in a tub, sink to the bottom, and require immediate resuscitation.

"There are showers here, you know," Bob says.

"Indeed there are. But LapLand has a certain je ne sais quoi. Not that I bathed there in the first place."

"I've never gone in that room the whole time I've worked here," Coffen says.

"You should. It's marvelous. Hey, is your ass hungry?"

"Sure."

"Sorry for cursing," Ace says. "I've got a problem with

it, and the problem is that I love cursing. It's a situation I'm aware of. How can I not be with the building manager, Mr. Winston, on my ass—I mean, sorry, my hind parts—every day about watching my mouth around the building's tenants. That means you. He thinks cussing is a bad habit. I think cussing—or 'the poetry of the streets,' as I like to call it—is more akin to the real world."

"Will you please cinch your robe?"

"The poetry of the streets is a beast in sheep's clothing," says Ace. "But don't egg me on. I have to stop using so many curses. My lady doesn't like it."

"Check."

"This is your lucky day," he says, very much not cinching his robe. "I'm making some of my renowned breakfast."

"It's nowhere near my lucky day."

"It's about to be. I am known for three things: One is shredding on the gee-*tarrrr*; the second is my glorious morning wood." Ace pauses and makes the international gesture for masturbation with his spatula-hand, moving it like mad in front of his pelvis. Then he does a little dance that's mostly running in place but with a sprinkle of cross-country skiing and lip-licking. "But the thing I'm known for that you shall currently reap the benefit of is my secret French toast recipe. I'll even let you in on it. Everyone loves Frosted Flakes. And everyone loves rum. So one morning it hit me, why not put Frosted Flakes and rum in my French toast batter? I mean, I'm going to enjoy them all for breakfast anyway. Why not combine all these ingredients into one super-food?"

Coffen momentarily forgets Ace's difficulties with the long-lost art of bathrobe-cinching, because that secret recipe sounds delicious. Some Frosted Flaked and rummed-up super-food might be what the doctor ordered, assuming the doctor is half-crazed and clad in a gaping bathrobe.

"That's quite a recipe," Coffen says.

"Bet your ass, Chump Change," says Ace. "Sorry, I meant, 'bet your hind parts.'"

"Chump Change?"

"That's what me and the other guys on the building's clean team call you. You're always getting things from the vending machines with dimes and nickels. It's a term of endearment."

"Clean team?"

"We don't like being called 'janitors.' Makes us feel like toe jam on the corporate totem pole."

So Bob hadn't been crazy all those times he thought the janitors—nay, the clean-team members—smirked when he stood making one of his hourly purchases. They got a giggle out of his prudent dispersal of pocket change, eh? *Well, excuse me,* Bob Coffen wants to tell Ace. *My blood sugar gets low, and don't forget that frugality is an admirable trait in some societies.*

"Does it make you guys feel better about your job?" Bob asks.

"What?"

"The toe jam thing."

"Exactly," says Ace. "We are the toe jam thing. I couldn't have said it better myself."

"You did say it."

Ace extends the bottle of rum up in the air and says, "To all the toe jam on all the totem poles all over the world! You're in our hearts always. You will not be forgotten." Then he guzzles rum.

"I'm going to the bathroom," says Coffen.

"Enjoy yourself," Ace says, still twiddling with the bottle of booze, "and breakfast will be served when you get back."

On his walk, Coffen texts his kids.

To Margot: *How's your morning? I think you're great.*

To Brent: *How's it hanging, amigo?*

It's only a ninety-second trip to the bathroom—take a leak, brush teeth with the plastic-bagged toothbrush, sans toothpaste, breath still stinky afterward, his tongue a hostel for transient bacteria. He sticks out his tongue to analyze it in the mirror. It's as if he can taste the acrid flavor that this might not be a blip with Jane, might be more than a one-weekend anomaly. The idea is globbed on his tongue along with the other germs. Jane has never asked him to sleep somewhere else before. What if Bob's life is changing and he barely gets a say in the matter?

Ace sets two paper plates down on the small table, also plastic forks. Coffen does get a non-plastic coffee mug filled with coffee, which makes the scene a bit less depressing.

"Shall we say a prayer?" Ace says.

"If you want."

"Please, Jesus, let my hair grow back. God, if there really is a god, why is the hair on my head falling out and the hair on my back growing like gangbusters? I mean, come on: I've gone *mano a mano* versus the world my whole life, so why can't I keep some freakin' hair as the fruits of all these labors?"

"Amen?" Coffen says.

"A-freakin'-men!" Ace claps his hands, then digs into his French toast. Bob follows his lead and cuts himself a bite with the edge of the fork.

There is no doubt that this is the single greatest bite of

French toast Coffen has ever ingested. Still chewing, he says simply, "Superb."

"Rum: the other white meat," says the trailblazing, bath-robed chef.

Which, of course, makes no sense, but Ace is smiling and so is Coffen, and why ruin a good moment, a great bite, with something boring and purposeless like sense?

"You and I," Ace says, "don't really know each other. For example, did you know that I'm in a Kiss cover band called French Kiss? Our singer is from Paris, and he can sing like Paul Stanley. Total dead ringer. There are a lot of schmucks out there playing Kiss songs exactly the way they were originally recorded. Which is fine. To each their own. But we have a secret weapon that those schmucks can only fantasize about. Our singer sings the songs in French. *In French!* As far as I know, we're the only Kiss cover band on the entire planet where the singer goes international, baby. That's what separates us from the packs of poseurs and wannabes."

"Sounds interesting," Coffen says, savoring each succulent chewing motion. He's also savoring all of Ace's inane blathering, more distraction from Jane booting him out.

"We may be old and balding and fat as hell," Ace muses, "but we can still rock and roll with the best of 'em."

Coffen has devoured his portion of breakfast, and he now sips his coffee. "If you opened a diner that served only this French toast, you'd be a very rich man."

"I do it for the buzz, not the glory."

"Honorable."

"Can I pry a bit?" Ace says.

"Why not?"

"Did you sleep here last night?"

"I fell asleep at my desk because I'm finishing up a new game design."

"Oh yeah, what game?"

"Scroo Dat Pooch."

"And it's about . . ."

"Pooch screwing."

"Not gonna tell you how to do your job, Chump Change," he says, "but is there a market for dog sex games?"

"Probably not."

"It's like rock and roll. You have to give the kids what they want. If you don't, you'll be banished to obscurity."

Something makes Bob feel like telling the truth. Maybe it's the rum. Maybe it's waking up on a beanbag. Maybe it's that Ace is staying here, too. "My wife threw me out last night."

"So did my girlfriend. Not last night. Wednesday."

"Why?"

"She wants to get married."

"You've been staying here since then?"

"Unofficially."

"I won't say a word to Dumper," Coffen says.

"We'll be roommates here."

In some way that makes Bob feel better—or again, the rum is kicking in. He checks to see if Brent or Margot texted back yet. Nada.

Coffen sends the same note to both of them this time: *I'm the luckiest dad in the world!*

"You're all right, Chump Change," Ace says.

Coffen thinks, *Why all these nicknames?* First, there's the plock praising Robert for all his years of faithful service. Then there's Tilda calling him the *capitán* of Mexican lasagnas and also a cop. Why doesn't anybody think of Bob as Bob?

"I am Bob," he says.

"You staying here all weekend?" Ace asks.

"Unfortunately."

"Are you going to mope the whole time or should we have some fun?"

"Probably I'll mope," says Bob.

"It's not going to do you any good. Mope when you're old. Tonight let's remember that we're lucky to be alive."

"I don't feel lucky to be alive."

"Well, you are—we all are—even those of us squatting at work. And my band is gigging tonight at Empire Wasted. You should come along."

"I think I'll stick with moping."

"Not a chance I'm letting you do that. Come on—get out of your head. Let's go out and live a little."

Coffen likes this idea of living a little. Maybe it's exactly what this house cat Robert Coffen needs—to get out of his head, get out of his latest game, get out and interact with somebody. "You know what? I'm in," Bob says. "Let's live a little."

"Rock and roll is quite the temptress. Few men can ward off her seductions."

"What instrument do you play in the band?"

"Do you even have to ask?"

So Coffen asks, "Why shouldn't I have to ask?"

"My nickname is Ace, as in Ace Frehley. I even got him tattooed on me," he says, rolls up his gaping bathrobe's sleeve and points at a picture of a guy with long straight black hair wearing white paint all over his face like a rodeo clown. There's black lipstick on him and also black patterns painted jagged around his eyes.

Coffen doesn't get it.

"He's the guitarist in Kiss—meaning I play guitar in French Kiss. I'm a straight-up shredder, a bona fide, certified, genuine genius of the fret board." Ace does his dance again: running in place and cross-country skiing and lip-licking, except now there's more flair to it.

Bob watches him shimmy and a smile crosses his face. Here's a guy, a core member of the clean team, who wants Coffen's company. Here's somebody who wants Bob around, and for a second he wonders, *When did I become so dispensable in my own life?*

Being included in Ace's plans makes Bob want to see his kids today, see his wife. He wants to get out and live a little in his own life, too.

The only thing that Coffen can choke out is this: "You really want me to be at your gig?"

"Bet your hind parts," says Ace.

■ Classic glory days shenanigans ■

Coffen isn't the kind of parent to put his kids in harm's way. So even if the alcohol present in the French toast mostly cooked off, Bob's not going to chance it. He feels a little under the influence, but maybe that might be placebo, or a by-product of a restless night's sleep on the beanbag. Problem is that if Bob's not comfortable operating a motor vehicle in his condition, then he needs to find an impromptu designated driver. Problem is that means his impromptu life coach, Schumann.

He needs somebody to drive him and the kids to the high-priced gym where Jane is training for her run at the world record. He needs to talk to her. Jane is at her most relaxed in the pool, which to Bob makes it the ideal time to chat.

Coffen's not really worried about being under the influence with just himself in the car, and so he chugs over to Schumann's to see if the maniac can be the DD.

It takes approximately four seconds for Coffen to regret this decision. He should have gotten a taxi, chartered a private jet, rented ponies, pogo sticks, whatever. Any other viable mode of transportation would have prevented Bob from being greeted like this in Schumann's foyer, Bob watching Schumann making growling angry-athlete faces.

"Have I lost it, Coffen? Is my face still the mask of a pigskin gladiator?"

"You look like a pigskin gladiator, I guess."

"I am a warrior."

"Schumann, I have real problems. I need to see my family. Can you give me a ride to my house to pick up my kids and then to the club?"

"It's like, I'm getting older and softer and weaker—and Charlie's out there in the bush, man. Charlie's squatting in the mud, staying sharp. Charlie's getting stronger."

"Who's Charlie?"

"Charlie from *Apocalypse Now*. The Viet Cong."

"How do you know somebody who was in *Apocalypse Now*?"

"Forget Charlie," says Schumann, getting really worked up. "He's not the point. I'm the point. I used to be sharp as steel. I was formidable. They used to have to game plan around stopping me. Now, what, I'm a guy who starts crying when you mention my kid? We were in the middle of heisting that magician and I started blubbering in the driver's seat. I'm pathetic."

His face goes slack of any glowering athletic snarls. Bob watches Schumann looking at himself in the mirror. Looking at himself the way you might look at a once-prized possession that was past its prime.

From Bob's perspective, having a face like Schumann would be a nice change of pace. Schumann keeps his hair in a buzz cut, like a throwback 1950s athlete. His rugged good looks are obvious: a jawline that tells everyone he can take a punch, a classic nose, and brown eyes that have no doubt taken a punch or two in their time.

"We weren't heisting that magician," Bob says. "You were."

Schumann slaps himself across the face. Hard. His cheek immediately goes pink. He shakes his head around and howls and says, "I can get my game face back. I'm not dead yet."

"What you did wasn't pathetic at all," Coffen says. "Your priorities have changed. And for the better, I might add. You care more about your family than you do for yourself."

"I won't wait for Charlie to crawl out of the jungle and slit my throat. So we tried to kidnap the magician and failed once. We won't make that mistake again, Bob. Next time, he's ours. I've been playing the game on the football field of my mind, and we'll be prepared for war."

"Where's your wife?" Coffen asks.

"She and little Schu are at that new aquarium. There's a sea horse show going. Then they're off to her sister's for a couple days. Not back until next week."

Maybe Coffen and his kids can take in the aquarium together. Might be a nice outing, and it's been a while since he's taken them to do anything fun. Plus, picking them up from the house might give him a chance to do some recon, assess the damage.

"We're basically without spouses this weekend," says Schumann.

"Don't remind me."

"Remind you? This is how Coach would draw it up. This is how we can get our mojo back. It's all about glory days, Coffen. We've stoked the renegade in my guts. He's awake and ready to rumble. I can relive the past. I bet you never even had any glory days, did you?"

"I had glory days."

"What happened in these alleged glory days of yours?"

"I stayed up pretty late. I drank my share of vanilla-flavored vodka."

"Those are the kind of glory days that give real glory days a bad name. My glory days would punch yours in the face and give them a swirly in the closest toilet. I bet part of it is the prestigious uniform. Speaking of that . . ."

"I also bowled a lot, and one time I stole the shoes," Coffen says. "That's a pretty crazy thing to do."

Then Schumann blurts, "Would you like to see me in the cloth of my tribe?" He does another snarl, wild in the mirror.

"The what?"

"The cloth me and my fellow warriors wore at Purdue University."

"I guess so."

"He guesses so," Schumann says. "This is the time to take what's ours. Victory is there, but nobody's going to give it to us on a shiny platter. We have to seize it! Are we going to seize the shiny platter of our rightful property of victory?"

"I still guess so," Coffen says.

And Schumann tears up the stairs, stomping about. Sounds like an animal running loose, say a raccoon looting garbage cans. Things are being thrown about above Bob. Schumann had been the one to ram Coffen into the oleanders, but now it seems the events of the last week might have run Schumann into his own set of merciless bushes, jarring him down some kind of wormhole in which he can slip into skin that's been dead for years.

It's not long before he's bounding down, taking the stairs three at a time, and jumping to the ground floor wearing his football getup—helmet, shoulder pads, cleats, the whole shebang—and he's screaming, "Now, is this the day we seize our shiny platter of our rightful property of victory or what?"

Inadvertently, Schumann is telling Coffen what he wants to hear. Bob does want his shiny platter of victory, only in this context, that's his family. "I need you to drive me to the pool."

"Wait, how did you get to my house?"

"I drove, but I can't drive my kids. I had some rum with breakfast."

"Rum in the morning. Nice. Now that's got glory days written all over it."

"Will you drive?"

"I thought Jane didn't want to see you," Schumann says.

"She probably doesn't. But I have the tickets Björn gave me to his next show. That should score me some points, even if she's pissed at first."

Schumann does one more growl and smacks himself on the shoulder pads, then the helmet. "Let's hit the field," he says.

■ ■ ■

Erma is obviously less than thrilled to see Bob, and says to him, "Didn't I tell you to call first?"

Bob's first thought: *This is what being a weekend dad will be like. I'll pick up the kids, take them on outings of phony camaraderie. They'll have a stepfather they admire more than me. And I'll eat hot dogs alone in an unfurnished apartment.*

"Yeah, sorry, my phone is dead," Coffen says to Erma. "I'm going to take the kids out for a while."

"Fine by me."

The kids, however, don't want to go to the pool. Brent is gaming in his room. Margot is glued to her iPad, exploring a crevasse at the North Pole with Ro. It's clear that bribery is the only arrow in Bob's quiver if he's to coax them to the pool this afternoon. Twenty bucks each, though he gets the sense that once Margot puts the pieces together—and she will; his daughter is whip-smart—she might change the stakes some, ask for her cut to be heightened in exchange for compliance, or she'll narc him out. The constant onslaught of Hollywood films has made children incredible negotiators.

It's a warm day. Seventy-one degrees. No wind to speak of. A meteorologist might call the conditions *suburban delight*.

Schumann takes the main drag across town. The Coffen kin are buried in their gadgets. Bob stares out the window. No Mom and Pop presence in this suburb, every business is a cut-out of a business that originated someplace else. The intersection the Coffens currently sit at is a paradise of saturated fats—fast food Chinese, two corporate burger joints, a fish-and-chips shop that originated in Seattle, and a Taco Shed. The latter makes Bob's stomach growl.

When they first moved here, Bob and Jane used the usual rationalization: Yes, this is a boring suburb, but the public schools are great and besides, it's only a half-hour drive into the city, which is true. They haven't, however, driven into the city in over a year. The freeway would take them there, if they got on it. The Coffens' universe is getting smaller every year, as confining as a snow globe.

The pool where Jane practices treading water is a component of a high-priced gym that costs Bob $650 a month. The facility actually has two pools: a pristine, immaculately maintained indoor facility, where the very serious swimmers are allowed to train. There are two members who are Olympic hopefuls in their respective strokes. There's an underwater ballerina who often hones her craft here. And, of course, Jane. These four represent the small caste permitted in the fancy indoor waters.

There's also an outdoor pool that's for the laypeople of all ages, the splashers, the elderly with their calisthenics, the Marco Polo players, the dog-paddlers, the pissers. This stratification between the two domains is strictly enforced.

The good news, at least from Bob's perspective, is that the indoor and outdoor pools are only separated by one gigantic window. So if he were to, say, insist that his children accompany him to the outdoor pool for a couple hours of wily water shenanigans, he'd be able to see Jane and Gotthorm getting their workout in prior to the big bid to break the world record.

Bob gets the kids settled by the outdoor pool, close to the lifeguard chair, though it's currently empty. Neither child is wearing a suit, though they have them packed in a duffel bag sitting between their chaise lounges. Schumann, also a member of this esteemed fitness community, stands there, still shoved into his whole football uniform.

"Dad," Brent says, pointing indoors, "I see Mommy!"

Margot makes a face: *You are busted*. Unlike her brother, she's pointing directly at Coffen.

Bob says to her, "Shall we make it $50?"

Coffen would like to think it's not greed that makes her ponder these new terms. He'd like to believe it's dedication—that his daughter, sensing something might be wrong between her parents—wants to help her dear old dad right the ship. This is what Bob would like to think, and he's doing a decent job convincing himself that it's probably true until Margot says, "$75."

"She's good," says Schumann.

"Deal," Bob says.

"I hate swimming," Brent says.

"Did you bring your phone, buddy?" Bob asks. "Play a game and sit here enjoying the afternoon. You don't have to swim."

"I want to go inside."

"Not right now. It's good to be outdoors. And we'll get frozen yogurt on the way home."

"People call it fro-yo, dad," Margot says, fiddling with her iPad, settling into her lounge chair.

"Fine, we'll get fro-yog after."

"Fro-yo."

"That's what I said."

"You said fro-*yog*."

"She's right," Schumann says. "We all heard you."

"I'll be right back," Coffen says. "Schumann, keep an eye on them."

■ ■ ■

Gotthorm is the first to see Coffen enter from the men's locker room and he shouts, "*Nei, nei, nei, nei!*" and waves his arms aggressively at Bob. He's of course wearing nothing but his Speedo, though he normally never swims—at least not that Bob has ever observed—so a swimsuit seems unnecessary. Instead, he stands on the deck, hands on his hips, giving Jane instruction and encouragement—and, of course, a lovely view of the bulge.

"I'm here for Jane," Coffen says, pointing to his wife, who bobs in the water.

"We can't have you here, Bob," Gotthorm says. "We need her mind flat as a frozen sea. We need her mind smooth and lithe."

"She and I are 'we,' Gotthorm. *We* are married."

"Not near the pool you're not. Here, Jane is not a person. Here, she is muscle memory. She has no active mind. She is seaweed."

"I don't have time for your Swedish philosophy."

"Norwegian."

"Same thing."

"Those two nations once fought a war. We're very different people."

"Yeah, who won?"

Gotthorm moves his arms in a dismissive gesture. "Jane is a drop of salt water. She is a molecule. She is the ocean and the ocean is Jane. No one can tell them apart."

"Then why's she in a chlorinated pool, genius?"

"Please go, Bob," Jane says, still treading water.

"But I have something for you."

"We'll talk after I go for the record. Give me these days to train, please."

"What I have for you won't wait that long," Coffen says.

"Then it's not that important," she says, coughing a bit from swallowing some pool water.

"That's your fault," Gotthorm says to Bob. "We don't cough. We don't break the flow of our gait until you arrive. We are a sea creature until you barge in."

Jane isn't looking. In fact, her eyes are closed. She seems to be done coughing, seems to be trying to find her center again.

"You go away," says Gotthorm. "Let us glide with the turtles. Let us drift in a current."

"I have something for Jane that's none of your business."

"Until we go for the record, everything is my business."

"I'm leaving these tickets with the Cro-Magnon, Jane,"

Coffen says, handing over the tickets to Björn's next gig to Gotthorm. "It's the magician's intermediate show. You were right. He can help us. I really want to go back and see. I want to fix us."

Jane doesn't open her eyes or answer.

"Did you hear me?" Bob asks.

"An eel can't hear a fool bellow from the shore," Gotthorm says. "A mollusk has no use for your codes of language." Then Gotthorm tucks the tickets in the front of his Speedo, dangerously close to the bulge, leaving only a short tongue of the tickets hanging out the top, like they're a couple of dollar bills wedged in a G-string at a strip club.

"Can you not get your genital warts all over those?" Coffen asks.

Gotthorm turns his back on Bob, focusing his attention on the pool, on Jane. Her eyes are still closed and she puckers her lips as she exhales big breaths.

"The show is on Sunday night," Bob says. "It will only take a couple of hours. It won't affect you going for the record on Monday. It might help. It might make you feel even mentally lighter if we're in a really good place as a couple."

Her eyes snap open, but she doesn't say anything.

Coffen tries to take that as a sign, but what does it mean?

Jane's lips still puckering as she breathes out.

Bob stands and watches for a few seconds, wordless.

She is beautiful, treading water there.

▪ Fro-yo hell ▪

The fro-yo shop is a swarming mess of children and unhappy parents. It's crammed with the aftermath of Saturday-afternoon soccer games; screaming teammates and rabid enemies now congregate here high on endorphins. They're either ecstatic with winning—*To the victors go the fro-yo spoils!*—or surly, grass-stained losers in need of sugary consolations to salve their suburban wounds of defeat.

There's a line of people out the door, waiting to order. The crowd is getting restless, collectively unimpressed with the amount of staff present to dispense this frozen elixir. Only one teenage girl toils behind the counter and she's overwhelmed. Surely, this isn't the first Saturday, post-soccer frenzy, so where are her coworkers? She's back there in a frothy fit, wearing a pink polo shirt and pink visor. Coffen can tell she's doing her best; he can clearly see that, and her effort makes him patient. He decides right then to stuff $5 in her tip jar.

"My manager had to go home early," the girl says to Bob, after he asks about her lone presence on such a popular shift. "She says she can't be nice to people today because Mercury is in major retrograde."

"I guess that makes sense," Coffen says.

Margot wants boysenberry swirled with French vanilla. Brent wants Dutch chocolate with gummy bears and crumbled Oreos as toppings. They seem intimidated by their soccer-clad colleagues. Neither has said a word since entering this congested fro-yo hell, both buried in their online lives. Maybe Bob should suggest organized team activities to them, see if they like getting grass stains all their own.

Schumann says he wants nothing except the chance to once more prove himself on the battlefield with the magician. Kids and parents alike stare at his football uniform.

"Let it go," Bob says to him.

"I hate losing."

"We didn't lose."

"Coach would tell me I lost. He'd say, 'You let me down, boy.' He'd say, 'How are you going to redeem your lackluster effort?'"

"And what would you say?"

"I would speak with ruthless actions," says Schumann.

■ ■ ■

They drop Margot and Brent off at home. Coffen guides them inside the house. Erma sees him and motors over to block his path in the foyer. "That's far enough," she says.

"Jane's not back?"

"They're strategizing," says Erma. "We did a very low-impact tread today, then the rest of the afternoon is working on mind-set."

Bob sighs and says, "'Bye, kids. Maybe we can go to the aquarium tomorrow. There's a sea horse show."

"Ro and I swam with sea horses last week."

"Where?"

"The Great Barrier Reef."

"These are real sea horses, though."

"They look exactly the same. I see them through glass here"—she shakes her iPad—"and we'll see them through glass at the aquarium."

"That's completely different, Margot."

"It is and it isn't."

"Real sea horses will be in real aquariums."

"My real phone contains real images of real sea horses really swimming. It's six of one, half dozen of the other."

Bob turns his attention to his youngest, asking, "Buddy? Aquarium tomorrow?"

Brent furrows. There's brown fro-yo smudged on his cheek. He says, "Only if I get past level seven before then."

"Okay, I'll call you in the morning."

"Text," he says.

"I'll text."

Bob walks back out of his light gray house. He notices the front lawn is getting a little shaggy—better get the gardener in line or the HOA will no doubt pelt him with belligerent emails. They pounced quickly when Coffen hung that bird-feeder a few months back without proper consent. How might his neighbors feel about the decorative contraption? wondered a passive-aggressive note sent from the HOA's commander-in-chief. What if everybody wanted to hang an unapproved birdfeeder out in front of their homes? Should such a slippery-sloped precedent be employed? One day, it might simply be birdfeeders, but what eyesores lurked around the corner? Pornographic statues? Could such a gamble possibly benefit the subdivision's greater good? A zero-tolerance policy had to be maintained.

A meteorologist might call the conditions *getting windier*.

Coffen's phone rings. The caller ID does not identify anyone he knows. Normally, he doesn't answer these mysterious numbers because rarely are they anything but veiled hassles, but he needs a friend—even a pesky solicitor, or a receptionist reminding him of an impending appointment, or a local delegate hoping to win his vote, whatever. He picks up on the second ring and says, "Bob is me?" not intending for it to sound like a question, but it does.

"What are you doing?" says some guy.

"Who is this?"

"This is a handsome member of the clean team."

"Ace? How'd you get this number?"

"You people have to remember that the clean team has access to everything. We don't only dump the trash. We have keys, alarm codes. We can get into every cranny. We know where you bozos hide your passwords and who has the best snacks tucked in desk drawers."

"What can I do for you?"

"I'm gonna go back to the office to hang out before the big gig," Ace says, "if you want to meet me there."

"Okay," Coffen says, excited to spend some time away from Schumann.

"If you're still feeling the effects of the rum, drive slow," he says. "Drunk drivers usually get popped for speeding."

"I'm not drunk driving."

"Exactly. No way would you. Remember to go slow. Before Acey settled down and joined the clean team, he might have wriggled on the wrong side of the law occasionally."

"Your glory days."

"Boy, were they."

"Right now my life feels like the opposite of glory days."

"We'll see what some rock and roll has to say about that later tonight," says Ace.

■ ■ ■

Bob has Schumann swing them by Taco Shed for an afternoon Mexican lasagna. They pull into the drive-through and Coffen almost tells him about Tilda's shady business venture, but he decides to keep her secret safe. She seems like a good person, and Bob wants her to make all the extra money she needs.

He does not, however, expect Tilda to be working the day shift, but he recognizes her voice right off. Apparently, one of the other workers is on maternity leave and the extra shifts have been disseminated amongst the remaining Shedheads.

"Hi, Tilda, it's Bob Coffen," he says from the passenger seat.

"Bob who?"

"Last night. With Otis."

"It's not ringing a bell."

"The cop."

"Still no."

"The *capitán* of Mexican lasagnas."

"Ah, yes," she says. "How many would you like?"

"Three." Coffen feels the urge to talk to her alone. He wants a couple minutes without Schumann here to chat. Bob truly enjoyed their time together last night, chomping Mexican lasagnas in the parking lot. He whispers to Schumann, "Give me a minute."

"Why?"

"I need to talk to her."

"Hark the herald angel likes to watch TV in his birth-day suit," Schumann says, smiling, parroting the magic words to get into Tilda's erotic speakeasy.

"Who's that?" Tilda asks.

"It's Schumann."

"Howdy, big fella," she says.

"You guys know each other?" Bob says.

Schumann only shrugs. Tilda says, "Don't be a prude, *capitán*."

"Can I talk to Tilda privately, Schumann?" Bob says. "Will you give me a minute?"

"Teammates can say anything in front of each other," Schumann says.

"Now, Schu, play nice. Give me and Bob a moment alone," Tilda says through the intercom.

Schumann makes a face like this is truly an inconve-nience for him, but quickly exits the driver's seat in a huff, slamming the door. Bob crawls over the center console.

"You okay?" Tilda asks.

"Never better," he says. "Except that's a lie."

"I've been better, too. Found out one of my exes is getting lethally injected soon. Turns out he's a serial killer."

Nothing from Coffen.

"Did you hear me?" Tilda asks.

"Why did you sleep with a serial killer?"

"It was an accident," she says. "He wasn't wearing any kind of identifying badge."

"Cops and monsters."

"Now you're catching on. Plus, he wrote poetry."

"What were they about?" Coffen asks.

"Mostly they were whiny anecdotes about how he needed more love in his life. He had a crappy father."

"Me, too," Bob says.

"Me, too," says Tilda. "The Mexican lasagnas are ready. Please pull up to the window."

"Before I pull up, can I ask you something?"

"Ask away."

"Do you ever want to get out of your box?"

"What box?"

"The box you're in right now," he says.

"I'm at work right now."

"Right, but I mean the box that our lives turn into, whether we want it to happen or not."

"Just break out of your box."

"I'm talking about being trapped," Bob says. "My life, my job, my wife. Jesus, my kids are in a box that I created for them—they barely go outside. They are more comfortable online. They're afraid of real life."

"Stop feeling sorry for yourself," says Tilda. "My daughter is in a literal box—Roy's car. Now that's a fucking problem."

She's right, Coffen thinks. *That's a problem.* He can fix what he's teaching his children, starting tomorrow, starting with the sea horses. They say they don't want to come, well, Coffen's going to make them come. He's their father. He'll insist, and if that doesn't work, the bribery from this afternoon might rear its ugly head again. He has the money and if that's the bait to get them to go, so be it.

"If you ever fancy a change of careers," Bob says, "I think you have a future in helping people."

"I do help people: Every time a guy pulls his pud while I talk dirty, that's helping humanity."

"You know what I mean."

"I do," she says, "but why would I give up all this glamour?"

Coffen pulls the SUV up to the window.

Tilda hands him the bag of lasagnas. He's astounded by her muscles every time he sees them, the way she's wrapped her heart in bulky protection. He looks across the parking lot and sees Schumann, uniform and all, throwing rocks at a stop sign. "He's one of your regulars?" Coffen asks her.

"That man loves him some raunch. If he wanted to take our relationship to the next level, I'd certainly get out of this box so he could get into mine."

"Do you like music?"

"What kind?"

"Kiss."

"I love Kiss," she says.

"I'm going to hear a Kiss cover band tonight. Wanna come with?"

"Are you asking me out on a date?"

It hadn't occurred to Coffen how this innocuously conceived question might be received. He meant nothing smarmy. The last thing on earth he wants is to cheat on his wife. Coffen posed the invitation to Tilda simply for the companionship, and in fact, the mere idea of an official date with her brings with it a few unfortunate images: He pictures Tilda's naked, engorged muscles, then the likelihood that if she ever saw Bob nude, the probability of her unbridled laughter.

"Not a date. As friends," Coffen says.

"Good. I don't date prudes. But as long as we're going as friends, I'd love to."

"I'm not a prude."

"Guess we're adding to our list."

"Our list?"

"Cops, monsters, and prudes," she says.

▪ Plucking and tightening ▪

Half an hour later, Coffen arrives at the office with a bottle of rum, ready to return the favor and get Ace nice and buzzed. But that plan won't work because Ace has company. Currently, Coffen's wedged in a cubicle near his work's kitchen, eavesdropping as Ace talks to a boy who looks about Margot's age. Who is this mysterious lad who's shown up with the tattooed janitor? Well, as Coffen has learned from his gutless spying, the boy happens to be the son of Ace's girlfriend. Apparently, Ace normally lives with his girlfriend and her son. The janitor has been sleeping at the office this week since she told him to "poop or get off the pot" regarding the likelihood of a marriage proposal.

"That was how she phrased it to me, dude," Ace says to the boy. "Your ma talks straight from the heart, and I love that about her. But she caught me off guard."

Ace relates all this to the lad as they sit at the kitchen table, the very place where Coffen had plunked down and enjoyed Ace's rum-soaked French toast. Ace has a guitar case across his lap, though he hasn't opened it. Then he says to the boy, "I mean, I love your ma. You know that. You see us together. You see how I make her laugh, and once you become a man, you'll realize there's no greater feeling than making the woman you love laugh like crazy. I needed a few days to sort things out on my own, and now I clearly know what needs to be done."

"Only a loser would sleep at his work," the boy says.

"It's a complex world, my man."

"My real dad has a condo in Memphis."

"Now that's a town that loves its music."

"My real dad owns his own plumbing business."

"Can I talk to you honestly, big guy? *Mano a mano?*" Ace seems unfazed by the boy's hostile words, which impresses Bob. It's no easy feat staying calm in the face of being demeaned. Not always easy to turn the other cheek if you know the next smack is coming.

Speaking of the next smack, Ace rubs his bald head, which prompts the kid to say, "Why don't you have any hair?"

"At your age, I had a coif."

"Will my hair fall out when I'm old?"

"Did your gramps have a good set of hair?"

"Which one?"

"Your ma's dad."

The kid looks petrified. "He was bald!"

"Then you too shall cross this humiliating bridge."

Coffen cracks the seal on the rum, holds it up to offer a commiserating cheers to the humiliating bridge of baldness, and has a slug.

Calm as can be, Ace opens the guitar case, pulls out the instrument, and lays it across his lap, loosening a string. He keeps talking, "I need to put some fresh strings on for the gig tonight. And on our way to the show, I'll take you for some Korean barbecue before we meet up with your ma. Who knew effin' Koreans could barbecue like kings, huh?"

The boy says, "I hate barbecue."

Ace nods and keeps winding a new guitar string tight. "Dude," Ace says, "this is an oddball world. Look around you, look outside—it's only getting weirder. I firmly believe that we should all boogie to our own beat. I'm a firm believer in fulfilling whatever destinies we want. I don't believe in God or any make-believe shit—sorry, I meant to say 'feces.' I don't believe in any of that. Do you forgive my swearing? Your ma hates my swearing and I'm working on it because I want to be a good partner and also a father figure. What I'm trying to say is that in life we should all make up our own rules. Make a world that's going to make us happy. I'm making up mine. I hope you're making up yours. I bring this up for a specific reason . . ."

Ace winds the next guitar string tight, the pitch of the string getting higher as he plucks it and tightens the tuning peg.

"My real dad thinks guitars are fucking stupid."

"You shouldn't swear either, dude. Your ma doesn't like it."

Plucking, tightening.

"Fucking stupid," the kid says.

"Anyway, here's the message I'm trying to send to you: I love your ma. She's the woman for me. I never thought I'd say that, never imagined myself settled down into the calm ballad of monogamy. But we change."

Plucking and the note bends higher . . .

Coffen has another slug of rum.

"Let me get down to brass tacks," says Ace. "I don't think it's a coincidence that we're here together right now."

The boy interrupts him. "You brought me here."

"Of course. I meant that more metaphysically."

"You picked me up from soccer and dragged me here."

"Yes, I did. I called your ma and said I had to talk with you man to man. See, dude, I've been wanting to ask your ma to marry me. But only if her son approves of our union. So your ma says, 'Poop or get off the pot.' That's what she's telling me, and I know the answer clear as day."

Ace is smiling at the boy.

The boy is not saying anything.

"The answer is that Acey shall poop," Ace says and smiles even larger.

"Shit wherever you want. I don't care," the boy says. "My dad might still come back someday."

"I don't have to tell you how awesome your ma is," Ace says. "I know you've had a hard life with your pops moving to Memphis. To be honest, Acey didn't exactly get the red carpet treatment himself. Look closely—that's not a silver spoon in my mouth, dude. It's a horse's bit. That was how my family treated me, like a dang animal with a bit in its mouth. You don't even want to hear about an unnamed boy named Ace whose dad liked to drag him to the racetrack with him, and sometimes the old man would get so tanked that he'd leave the boy behind, this unnamed boy named Ace, forced to fend for himself until his mom finally drove to the track to pick him up. So be sure that I know hard living. I know parents who shouldn't be allowed to have library cards, let alone children. And your pops splitting town . . . Jesus H, what a bastard, not that I want to speak ill of your flesh and blood. But I feel terrible for you. Your whole world was turned upside down. You're brave for marching on. But right this second, I have to tell you, I'm glad my path crossed with you and your ma's. I am glad we give each other shelter."

"You freeload at our house," the boy says.

"I think of it as being the house where we all live."

"Then why are you sleeping here?"

Coffen can barely stand the mouth on this smart-ass kid. He needs to get yelled at, or spanked, or water-boarded. He needs consequences. It makes Bob thankful for the manners of his own children. Jane would never let them speak that way. She's such a good mother. He has another slurp of rum.

Ace says, "This conversation is giving me the strength to come out and say it. It's important to me that this is okay with you. I want your blessing, dude. I want to know that you see this as a good thing. It's what she wants. We're happy. I'm good to her. Please tell me that we have your blessing."

Ace is plucking and tightening with another bending note moving higher. He looks hopefully at the boy, waiting for a blessing. He's right about it being an oddball world.

"Tonight at the show," he says to the boy, "I'm going to call her onstage and ask her to marry me. I haven't even told the guys in the band. I want everybody to be surprised. Except you and me. We will know what's coming. What do you think of all that?"

"Your band sucks."

"This is a lot to ingest, I know."

"Asking her to get married at your shitty concert is a shitty idea."

"I'm not trying to replace your dad, my man. I want to be a good husband to your ma. She deserves that. And I bet me and you can become pretty good friends if you decide to give me a chance."

Nothing from the boy. Just the stink-eye.

"Blink once if you caught the gist," Ace says.

"Barry hates his stepdad. Barry says stepdads are bullshit."

"Sure, some stepdads suck."

"Why do you give a fuck what I think?" the boy asks.

Ace still has the huge smiley face. "Because you're important to me."

"Fine, ask her," the kid says. "I don't care what you guys do anyway."

"Thanks, my man. I'm thrilled to have your blessing." He says this with no bitterness or sarcasm. He says this with sincerity. Bob can't believe it. This kid tried everything to rattle Ace and he only wound his strings, kept his cool. Coffen needs to remember that. Needs to remember the beauty of calm discourse. Ace told the boy exactly what was on his mind, the plain, whole truth, never getting side-tracked or rattled. That's what Bob has to do with Jane: honesty without resorting to Gotthorm cracks. Honesty without self-sympathy. Honesty without playing the martyr. Honesty without irony.

Another guitar string tightening. Ace must be paying more attention to the boy than the guitar. The skinniest string gets higher and higher and its pitch goes too high because the thing snaps, and Ace says, "Damn. Dang, I mean. You gotta pay attention or things break on you. Am I right, my man?"

Ace starts over, winding a new string to replace the busted one.

Bob staggers into the kitchen with the rum.

Ace and the kid look over at him.

The plucking and tightening stop.

Ace giggles. "Hey, Chump Change, what's with the long face?"

Coffen doesn't want to be alone any longer. He's crying, but he can't care about that. Things do break if you're not watching. He asks, "Can I get Korean barbecue with you guys?"

"Our entourage," says Ace.

▪ Three happy Kiss-loving clams ▪

"Tell me the name of a genius," says Ace, eating meat off the bone while sitting in a booth at Korean barbecue with Coffen and the boy. The restaurant is pretty empty. It's about an hour before they have to be at Empire Wasted for sound check.

"I don't give a shit about geniuses," his girlfriend's kid says.

"Shakespeare," Bob says.

"Koreans are meat-Shakespeares," Ace says.

"That's racist," the boy says.

"It's a compliment."

"It's still racist."

"Come on, name a genius."

"No," the boy says, "your racism is ruining my appetite."

"Einstein," Bob says.

"Koreans are Meat=MC²," says Ace.

"It's racist because you're making a generalization about a whole group of people," the boy points out.

"It can't be racist to celebrate the Koreans' meaty geniusness," Ace says. "I refuse to believe that. And if it is, then lock me up and throw away the meat-key because I'm a racist for how much I love freakin' Koreans! Name another."

The boy is mum.

"Michael Jordan," Coffen says. Hearing Ace and the boy banter makes Bob think of Brent, so he texts his youngest: *I miss you very much. You are a terrific son.*

Then Bob sends the same message to Margot, forgetting to change the word "son" to "daughter."

Within three seconds, she texts right back: *I'm a girl. Thankz for noticin*

Coffen: *Yeah, but you get the main message, right? The "you are terrific" part?*

R u guyz divorcing?

No

STFU

What's that mean?

Shut the eff up

You are a terrific daughter. Sea horses tomorrow?

She never answers, probably enjoying the Great Barrier Reef from the comfort of her bedroom.

"Koreans slam-dunk their meat like Mr. Mikey Jordan!" Ace says, suddenly an advertising exec, setting back international relations with every new slogan.

"This tea is terrible," Coffen says, putting his phone in his pocket.

"Drink beer, for god's sake," says Ace. "We're on our way to a rock and roll show, and you're totaling tea? Grow a pair, Bobby-boy. Let down the eight hairs you have left and live a little. Go *mano a mano* versus the world."

In Coffen's opinion, Bobby-boy does not need to grow a pair. It's true that he will soon be switching to beer, not because Ace peer-pressured him into it, but due to the fact that Korean tea is horrible. Now that's something worth being racist about.

"Tonight I ask your beautiful ma to be my lawfully

wedded wife," Ace says to the boy. "I'm thrilled to have your blessing, dude."

The boy frowns at Ace.

"What's wrong?" Ace asks.

"Nothing's wrong."

"You can tell me, my man. I know this is hard for you. Go ahead—put the screws to Uncle Acey. I can take it. You won't scare me off. Me, you, and your ma are going to be good together."

The boy's frown fades.

Is that a small smile?

Yes, indeed, the boy small-smiles at Ace and now the kid says, "Ace Frehley from Kiss."

"Are you saying Ace Frehley is a genius?" asks Ace, looking like he might start sobbing with oodles of pride.

Coffen's phone vibrates, alerting him that there's a new text, hopefully from Brent, hopefully confirming a father-son date to the sea horses. After watching Ace struggle with this boy, the task that Coffen has is easy—encourage some other activities besides gaming. Get Brent out of the house. Do stuff together. He can game, too, just not every waking second.

But the text isn't from Brent.

It's from Schumann.

And it is not good news.

It's what might be called the opposite end of the spectrum from good news.

Schumann texts: *Bagged me a magician.* ☺

Bob: *?*

Stalked him and secured him.

Why?

Tied him up and stuffed him in the back of the SUV.

Tied up??

Like a turkey.

Let him go!!

Where R U?

Coffen: *Meet me at Empire Wasted in 45.*

That sad dank bar that doesn't have any big screens? ☺

45 mins!!

Hut, hut, hike are the final words texted from Schumann.

"Do you mind if one of my friends meets us at the club?" Coffen says to Ace.

"You already said your friend from Taco Shed was coming."

"Her, too. This is my neighbor, Schumann."

"You're doing French Kiss a favor, helping us fill every seat in the house. The more, the merrier," Ace says, and then he looks at the boy again. "Like our household, right, dude? We're three happy Kiss-loving clams."

"Happy fucking clams," the boy says, which makes Bob think of his household: Would they be considered four unhappy clams, their shells boxing them away from everything in the world, much like the subdivision's electric fence?

Dumping salt in Coffen's wound, Ace starts humming *here comes the bride, here comes the bride . . .*

■ ■ ■

The three of them roll into Empire Wasted before Schumann or Tilda arrive. Coffen dismisses this place, shaped like a big rectangle, as a dump. The walls are stacked cinder blocks, neither painted nor covered, only nude gray concrete. The stage is pretty low to the ground with an empty dance floor in front of it. No tables anywhere. There's a bar at the back of the room. An old man behind it wearing a tank top. Bald on his head but not on his shoulders.

Bob helps Ace carry his amp in. Coffen is amped himself, paranoid-thinking about a kidnapped magician who's probably mighty pissed and ready to cast some nasty curses or, worse, call the cops and rat them out, not solely for Schumann's solo kidnapping tonight, but also for what he and Bob did to the magician last night.

Empire Wasted technically isn't open yet. The only people there are the staff, the band—the rest of French Kiss's chubby, bald members setting up gear—groupies, if you can call them that, and a few friends.

Coffen makes his way to the bar to order a beer and another text from Schumann comes through: *The eagle has landed.*

Which makes no sense to Bob, who responds simply with: *?*

Code for I'm out front.

So Coffen gets going out front. Sure as sure can be, there's crying Björn hog-tied in the back of the SUV, not pleased with the whole kidnapped situation that's unfurling before his eyes.

"This can't be good," Coffen says. "We're going to get shipped off to prison for round-the-clock sodomy sessions."

"In the right hands, sodomy can be beautiful."

"That's not really what we're talking about," Bob says.

"I have made a breakthrough," says Schumann, still wearing his football uniform, although thank god for small miracles, he's not wearing the helmet.

"Breakthrough with what?"

"I know what my gladiator identity was missing. I needed to stop using my white man name."

"You are white."

"I was. Or maybe I am normally, but not right now. Not while I'm wearing the cloth of my tribe. I'm a Native American warrior."

"I don't think so," Coffen says.

"From this moment on, I'll only answer to the name Reasons with His Fists."

"I refuse to call you that."

It looks like Schumann might start arguing with Coffen, but Björn makes these really angry mumbling noises.

"How did you even do this to him?" Bob asks.

"That show you saw last night. He did the same one tonight. So I waited outside and then snuck up and cold-cocked him and tied him up and taped his mouth and here we are."

"He's going to kill us."

"We scored a touchdown."

Coffen, once worried about being a weekend dad, now is crippled by fear that he'll be a prison dad, rotting away in a cell, scribbling letters that his children never respond to. They'll certainly never visit him. Prison dad doesn't spend holidays surrounded by loved ones. He spends them slow-dancing with his cell mate, resting his head on a muscled, tattooed shoulder.

"I'll never see Margot's graduation," says Bob. "Somebody else will explain the birds and the bees to Brent."

Schumann points at Björn: "We are the winners. I beat your ass, sucka!"

"I never asked you to do this," Bob says.

"We went for the jugular and were handsomely rewarded," Schumann says.

"What are you talking about?"

"The killer instinct of competition."

"That's exactly what I'm worried about, Schumann. What if he *kills* us once we let him go? What if he takes back his word about not calling the cops and he tells them everything?"

"I am Reasons with His Fists," he says, "and I fear no man."

"You are Schumann, and you should fear that man," Coffen says, pointing at the wiggling magician, still making angry mumbling noises.

▪ You are my testes-hero ▪

Bob Coffen flees Schumann and goes back in Empire Wasted to figure out what to do about Björn. He decides a beer is in the cards, goes over toward the stage once he consumes it in four panicked swigs. Ace is talking with a woman, presumably his girlfriend. The boy is hugging her. She pats his back.

"Here he is," says Ace and points at Coffen, by way of a weird introduction.

"Bob is me," Bob says to the woman, shaking her hand, watching the other one still patting on the boy.

"I'm Kathleen. Call me Kat."

"Very nice to meet you."

"Told you he was all manners," Ace says.

"Are you excited for the show tonight?" Coffen asks her.

"No matter whether me and Ace are fighting," Kat says, "I never miss a French Kiss concert. They are incredible, and Ace loves playing music so much."

Bob is impressed with Kat's commitment to Ace even when they're fighting—fighting to such an extreme that he's sleeping at work. "You are a good woman," Coffen says. "Sometimes people who you want to support don't want you around them. Sometimes they say that their Norwegian coach is the only team they need."

"What?" Kat asks.

"Let's cool it with the moping," Ace says to Bob. "We're here to live a little, right?"

■ ■ ■

Soon, Tilda saunters into the bar. She sees Coffen right off because the place is pretty empty. He's hunkered alone at the bar. Ace and the other members of the French Kiss contingent are all backstage putting makeup on one another's faces, getting into their facsimiles of Kiss characters.

Bob has switched from beer to vanilla vodka.

And he's well on his way to being intoxicated. If intoxication is like putting on a pair of pants, Coffen has one leg in for sure and is now working the other through.

Bob is so happy to see Tilda. Can Coffen call her a friend? He's going to. She chose to come here and spend time with him and that's what friends do, after all—they enjoy each other's company. Or so Bob's heard around the water cooler.

Tilda's wearing a cotton tank top and tight jeans. Muscles galore. Tanned muscles making lumpy stacks on her shoulders. She could be a cage fighter. In fact, Coffen doesn't know for sure that she isn't a cage fighter, so the first vanilla-vodka-atrophied idea that escapes his mouth is "You ever kill a man with your bare hands?"

"Always wear gloves because these days with all the DNA technology, killing with your bare hands is like signing a confession."

"Is that a metaphor?"

"Which part?"

"The whole thing."

"Sure," she says.

"I need to believe you haven't killed a man with your bare hands."

"Then why'd you ask the question?"

It's here that Coffen decides to enlist this bawdy Taco Shed confidant into Schumann's kidnapping ring. Why would he do such a thing? Why involve anyone else? Simply put: He's telling her because he's buzzed and feeling useless and like an outcast, a looming divorcé, a weekend dad destined to fail his kids (and that's not even to mention the terrifying prison dad hallucination), or to be replaced by somebody new, someone like Gotthorm—a man of strong body and mind, one blessed with a severe, Nordic bone structure, one well over six feet tall who can breed a platoon of bloodthirsty Vikings. This avalanche of panic isn't all that's going on inside Bob. Add to this the scene he's recently witnessed at Korean barbecue: the boy who'd been so cruel to Ace suddenly saying that Ace Frehley is a genius; the boy meeting Ace somewhere near the middle, compromising, extending an olive branch of sorts. Will that smart-ass kid do everything in his power to put Ace through the ringer during his teenage years? No doubt about it. But it was touching to see some effort from the boy tonight. Maybe that's all anybody's really after: effort. A stab to meet in the middle. All of this piles on Coffen's shoulders, plus the simple fact that there is a kidnapped sorcerer outside and Bob has no idea what to do next.

And so Coffen spills the beans to Tilda: "I'm tangentially involved in criminal activity this evening."

"Guess you're not the prude I pegged you for."

"You know how you used to think I was a cop?"

"I'm still on the fence."

"Really?" Coffen says, his feelings growing even more wounded. "Why?"

She nods. "I have trust issues. And if you are a cop, we're back standing on the fertile soil of entrapment."

"What if I was to say that I can prove I'm not a cop right this very second beyond any reasonable doubt?"

"That sounds like something a cop would say. Are you drunk?"

"Probably," he says, taking another swig of vanilla vodka, "and I'd like to let you in on my crime, if you'd be interested in such information."

"I'm listening."

"What we did was—"

"Wait, who's 'we'?"

"I'm talking about me and Schumann."

She smiles mischievously. "Schumann's here?"

■ ■ ■

He takes her out front to Schumann's SUV, which is still parked in the same spot as before, which was where Schumann had promised to leave it while Bob went back in the bar to formulate some kind of crackpot plan to deal with Björn, though once alone it occurred to Coffen that a) Schumann probably won't listen to his plan anyway, seeing as how he went ahead and swiped Björn on his own quarterback accord, and b) he kidnapped a master of the dark arts without any concrete idea what to do with him, simply stole him for some kind of contorted notion of victory, and c) nowhere in Schumann's cranium does there seem to be ample fear over the very real possibility of incarceration, and d) Schumann might be mentally ill or so hardwired for competition that he's somehow untrained for civilian life.

Coffen and Tilda approach. Schumann exits the driver's seat, walks toward the back but doesn't open it, keeping Björn obscured.

"Hello, big fella," Tilda says to Schumann, ogling his football uniform, the implied musculature underneath his sporty shell. "I was hoping our paths would cross when I wasn't working."

"I've changed my name to Reasons with His Fists," he says.

"Your name's as meaningless as these jeans I'm wearing," says Tilda.

"I'm married."

"Let's not ruin our first non–Taco Shed impression with too many details from our personal lives," she says.

"You'd make a good running back," Schumann says to her. "You see an opening and hit the hole hard, hoping to score."

"You're going to make me blush, Reasons with His Fists," she says.

"We need to focus," Coffen says inconsequentially.

"My name is a tribute to my tribe," Schumann says.

"Are you part Native American?" she asks.

"I am a warrior ready to ravage at the drop of a hat."

"I'm prepared to drop much more than my hat," says Tilda, enhancing her flirty words with a fellatio-impersonation, her hand moving back and forth in front of her open mouth. She looks like a demented sex-ed teacher trying to scare the kids into abstinence.

Schumann watches the demo and smiles. "You have the body of a fearsome warrior, too."

"I've taken my lumps over the years."

Coffen can't take his inconsequentialness any longer and throws open the back of the SUV. The three of them stand, staring at the squirming, angrily mumbling magician.

"Who's that guy?" Tilda asks, cool as a sociopath.

"Our vanquished foe," says Schumann.

"He looks pretty pissed," she says.

"His arms are probably asleep," Schumann says. "Not to mention I had to knee his testes to properly subdue him before pitching him in there."

"I like the way you say 'testes,'" Tilda says. "Can I hear it once more, except this time, make it a little breathier, like you're seducing me?"

Schumann answers in a baritone Don Juan playboy voice, "Testeeeeez."

"You are my testes-hero," she says.

"Anyway, this is the guy we kidnapped," Coffen says.

"I am your testeeeeez-hero," Schumann says, sexy voice doused with aftershave and five o'clock shadow.

"Maybe I'll wait for you guys in the bar," Coffen says, already sulking.

"That's a great idea," Tilda says. "Maybe Reasons with His Fists would like to take me for a drive so we can get to know each other more intimately. What do you say, daddy?"

"This will be like the glory days," Schumann says. "Pillaging a coed to mark an important victory. Hail Purdue!"

"Nobody's called me a coed in years," Tilda coos.

"What about him?" Coffen asks and points at squirming Björn.

"He'll be fine," she guarantees. "He might even enjoy the show." Tilda winks at Bob and then walks over and gets in the SUV via the passenger's side. Shrugging, Schumann hops back in, too, and starts the engine.

Coffen traipses up to his window and says, "I think we should deal with the problem at hand."

"We'll troubleshoot soon," Tilda says.

"I was talking to Schumann."

"Do you mean my new friend Reasons with His Fists here?" she asks.

"Yes," Schumann says, "who is this Schumann you keep referring to?"

"Don't encourage him," Coffen says to her.

"I'm a gal hoping to take a relaxing ride with a friend."

"He has a family."

"And I have a daughter, who's partial to living in Roy's car."

Making zero headway with Tilda, Bob turns his attention to Schumann, saying, "What about your wife?"

He revs the engine.

"You're not seriously about to drive off," Coffen says.

Then Schumann seriously drives off with Tilda giddy in the passenger seat.

■ A couple of pickling rocket scientists ■

Bob Coffen's been journeying toward intoxication and he's arrived at it. He's—as the bar's name publicizes—empirely wasted.

Schumann and Tilda have been gone now for half an hour. The bar is filling up. French Kiss is due to perform soon. Bob is alone, feels dusted in fluorescent orange. Like the artificial stuff is contagious and everyone's keeping their distance. Don't shake his hand, keep clear when he coughs. Otherwise, you might contract your own case, leaving you an estranged laughing stock. Too pitiful for pity. Too predictable for surprise.

The evening's mission to go out and live a little is turning out to be a failure. Maybe he's best at building games, best sequestered from the rest of humankind. Best suited for weekend dad status. Best living in a condo in Memphis. Best letting Gotthorm train his children in preparation for adulthood. He thinks about Ace's guitar string snapping, how things break if you're not watching out. What did Bob expect? Who'd been making sure things weren't about to snap in his family?

Kat prances up to Coffen, places her hand on his elbow, a welcome steadying: "Ace wants to know if you'd like to be backstage with all of us."

"I'd love to."

"You don't look so good. How drunk are you?"

"You look good, too. Is your hair naturally curly?"

"Have some water," she says.

■ ■ ■

The members of French Kiss are dressed like the real Kiss. Their makeup is very convincing. In fact, they are a very convincing lot, clad in black leather, platform boots. To a layman like Coffen, if they were lined up next to the original band, he wouldn't be able to distinguish between them.

Ace says to Bob, "Get ready, because French Kiss is about to rock your eyeballs loose from your heads. I'm telling you, we are fantastic. You won't believe it."

"Dude," the drummer says to Ace, "I get so inspired when you talk about rock and roll. You love it so much. I feel like I'm wearing some serious jealousy-cologne when you talk like that."

"Jealousy-cologne?" Ace asks.

"The musk of envy," the drummer says.

Apparently, Coffen isn't the only person whose bacchanalia has gotten the best of him, because now Ace says, "Keep drinking that coffee, Javier. Sober up. You hearing me? You can't keep pulling this shit. I mean, feces. Stop with the feces, Javier. Let your feces go the way of the dodo."

No one answers, so presumably Javier is not hearing him.

"Javier is more wasted than you are, Bob," says Ace.

"Who's Javier?"

"Him," Ace says and nods toward a sleeping guy sitting in a folding chair and leaning his head against a wall, a coffee wedged between his legs. Despite his compromised sobriety, Javier's Kiss makeup looks fantastic. "He's our bassist. Showed up cooked out of his skull. Rock and roll can be a tiring mistress."

"Will he be able to play?" Kat asks Ace.

"My queen," Ace says, "they say that the show must go on, but I've never heard them say that Javier's amp must go on. We'll prop him up. We only need him to stand there. So we've got that loophole to exploit if his condition doesn't drastically improve. We'll make it work one way or another."

"I've missed you," she says.

"And I've missed you," he says.

They kiss. There's a kinetic energy between them that Coffen is immediately envious of, resentful of. It's an energy that he's not sure he ever had with Jane.

For ten minutes all is well.

Then Javier wakes up. Then he throws up on the floor. Then he threatens to leave, spastically saying that he's thinking about quitting French Kiss forever because they don't respect his hot chops on the bass and maybe he'll take his talents elsewhere unless his prowess gets a bit more recognition.

"We recognize your prowess," Ace answers on the band's behalf, "but if I'm speaking honestly here, your chops are only lukewarm. You are proficient on your instrument, no doubt, but let's keep it real. A genius you are not."

"You shouldn't be under any delusions of grandness, bro," says the drummer to Javier.

"Grandeur," corrects the French singer.

"I'm a native English speaker, dude," the drummer says, "and your ass is writing checks your mouth can't cash."

"Respect my hot chops!" Javier screams, knocking his coffee over to mix with his vomit.

Javier is probably not going about this the right way, Bob thinks, but doesn't everyone want to have their hot chops recognized?

Javier rants on, "I'm out of this hellhole. You guys try playing this gig without me. Let's see how you fare without an artist of my magnitude. Let's see if anybody even wants to hear this band without my hot chops highlighting the action."

He stands up to go, slips in his vomit/coffee.

"Dude, we need you," says the drummer. "Don't do something you're going to regret tomorrow."

"Javi, just relax, bro," the French singer says.

"We pride ourselves on bringing the rock to the people," Ace reminds all. "If you leave now, we have to cancel the gig, and French Kiss does not cancel. Grandness, grandeur, whatever—don't make us flake on the show. Don't make us out to be liars to our legions of loyal fans."

"Adios, you who fail to recognize talent when it's waved right in your faces," Javier says and stomps out of the room.

The other bandmates follow after him, leaving only Coffen, Kat, and her son in the backstage dressing room.

At least for a few seconds . . .

Then Kat says, "I'm going to get a mop for that," motioning at the vomit/coffee and walking out.

Just Bob and the boy . . .

He looks at Coffen, which makes Bob nervous, especially after the venomous things Bob heard him say to Ace back at the office. But Bob also heard what he said at Korean barbecue, something nice, something sweet, so he tries to talk with him. "How old are you?"

"Twelve."

"So's my daughter. My son is nine. I can't go home this weekend."

"I bet they think you're a douche bag," the boy says.

"You're probably right."

"I only met you awhile ago and I think you're a douche bag."

"I'm not big on you, either. You should be nicer to Ace."

"Mind your own fucking business."

"He's only trying to make you guys happy."

"Why can't you go home?"

"Because I did some dumb stuff."

"Like what?"

"Bob is me."

"That's a douche bag answer," the boy says.

"I'd like to see you talk like that in front of your mom."

"I'm not fucking afraid."

"We'll see."

Kat wheels a mop bucket in, does the dirty work, slowly wiping the vomit/coffee up.

"I think your son wants to tell you something," Bob says.

"What is it, baby?" she asks the boy.

"I love you," he says.

"I love you too," she says.

The boy flips Bob the bird while she keeps mopping.

"Did Javier leave?" Coffen says to her.

"They're out there begging him to stay. He needs to go to rehab. Plain and simple. He's always doing things like this for attention. Did you drink your water? You should finish that water. What were you two talking about while I was gone?"

"He did something dumb," the boy says.

Satisfied that she's swabbed the decks clean, Kat puts the mop back in the bucket. "What did you do?" she says.

"I embarrassed myself in front of my wife," he says and starts crying. "She kicked me out of the house."

The boy laughs. "Look at the crybaby."

"Shh," Kat says to him. Then to Bob: "You shouldn't drink alcohol when you're in a bad place. It only makes things worse. I'm sure she'll take you back. Ace speaks very highly of you."

"Why should she take me back? I mean, what do I offer her? When was the last time I was actually interesting?" Bob says, and his sobs really get cranking.

"Please don't cry."

Despite Kat's pleas for him to stop, the booze and the agony have slithered themselves into a kind of astonishing knot and now that Coffen has given in, there's no stopping it—the liquor is a lubricant to tease out what had previously been dammed.

"We'll give you your privacy," she says.

"I'd love it if you stayed."

"That's okay."

"Please?" he says.

"We need to check on Ace," Kat says and ushers the boy out.

Bob is left alone with the mop bucket. Left alone with his memories, not just of this weekend but everything: all the bundled up personal experiences, labeled and ignored like cardboard boxes in a garage. Jane is sick of him. His kids barely notice him. It reminds Bob of his own childhood, the divorce he observed. Coffen can't allow himself to be the same absent father.

■ ■ ■

When he was a kid, Coffen's mom made the world's best fermented dills. Not that she only pickled cucumbers. No, she did all kinds of fruits—peaches and cherries and plums and nectarines. In the few months after Bob's dad first left, Coffen's mom didn't much feel like cooking meals that emphasized all four food groups and so she and Bob hunkered in the garage in beach chairs in front of her pickling fridge and ate whatever vinegary fruit tickled their fancy.

Across the back wall of the garage were the boxed-up memories. Not the stuff that belonged to Bob's dad. No, in the first days after he left, Bob's mom swerved around the house, throwing everything that reminded her of her husband into boxes and stacking them in the garage. By the time she was finished, their house had been pared down severely. Even the television had been boxed up, though Bob was able to convince her to get it back out again.

"Do you know what we are?" she said one night as they sat in front of the pickling fridge.

"What?"

"We're a couple of pickling rocket scientists."

"What's that?"

"Rocket scientists are probably the smartest people in the world. And no one knows more about pickling than us. So we're a pair of pickling rocket scientists."

"Cool."

"What's on the menu tonight, garçon?" she asked.

"What did we have last night?"

"Cherries."

"Then not cherries."

"What will it be?"

"Nectarines?" Coffen said.

"A fine choice."

She stayed slumped in her beach chair while he went to retrieve the nectarines from the pickling fridge. It was always Coffen's job to grab whatever jar, which meant he had to get close to the plums, their likeness to human hearts always scary. Like they'd been cut from their chests and dropped into spicy brining solution, saltier than tears.

Coffen tried to open the jar but couldn't. Brought it over to her and she cracked the seal. "Would you like to do the honors and taste the first bite?" she said and handed it back to him. "I'm not all that hungry tonight, garçon."

She only had four bites of cherries last night, and Coffen knew that without some prodding, she'd barely have any tonight, too. "You need to eat."

"That's what they say, but I haven't been this skinny since high school," she said. "We should tell the world about the pickled fruit diet. Get everyone in shape. Honestly, I've lost eleven pounds since he left."

Coffen stuck a fork in the jar and impaled a nectarine, then took a bite off it. Vinegary juice dripped down his hand and wrist, which he licked off, running his tongue all over his forearm.

"Fancy manners," she said.

"We're out of paper towels."

"Bon appétit, I guess."

"Bon appétit," he parroted back.

"Sorry I can't cook right now."

"These are good."

"I'll get it together soon."

"Want some?" Coffen held his nectarine-on-a-fork out to her, offering it with a hopeful smile. And it was a sincere expression. He meant that smile. The American Medical Association might not have pimped this skewered nectarine dinner as a rounded meal, but Coffen could not have cared less: These were happy memories, the two of them together on the beach chairs in the garage.

Happy memories don't have to be of happy times.

Bob's mom took the forked nectarine back from him and bit a small bite, mostly nibbling skin. "Bon appétit," she said again. "The chef highly recommends it. The chef has guests from all over the country come to dine on this delicacy."

"You already said that."

"Oh."

"Will I see Dad again?"

"Now I remember saying that. Sorry."

"Will I see him soon?"

"My mind is jumpy right now."

"When?"

"He'll come to his senses. You don't leave your family. He knows that. Everyone knows that." Coffen's mom smiled at him without much conviction. Then she added, "For our next course, can we have a plum? I'm in the mood for something sweeter. I didn't already tell you that, did I? I'd hate to think I'm retreading all my material tonight." She handed the stabbed nectarine back to Bob.

Obviously, he didn't want to go to the fridge and fetch a jarred plum, the fruit that reminded him of harvested hearts. But the idea of getting his mom what she wanted was more important to him. She needed to eat. Eleven pounds was too much weight to lose. A bite of cherries and a nibble on nectarine skin was no way for her to take care of herself.

Coffen peeked in and grabbed the jar. He was able to open this one on his own, the seal popping. Then he lodged a fork in the heart and handed it to her.

"He could come back soon," she said and took a bite of it, which made him feel great, seeing her eat something.

"He could come back tomorrow," Coffen said.

She nodded.

"He could come back tonight," Coffen said.

"You never know," she said, handing the plum to him, but he didn't dig in; he was too excited.

"He might be parking the car right now out front," Coffen said. "Right?"

She slunk down a bit in her beach chair.

"What do you think, Mom? Couldn't he be parking?"

"I doubt it."

"Maybe I'll go out front and look. Do you think he's out there?"

"Anything's possible," she said.

"Can I go check?"

"If you want."

"I hope he's out there," Bob Coffen said, holding and finally eating the heart.

Now, sitting with the mop bucket, sitting miles away from his wife and kids, it's hard for Coffen not to think that this is rock bottom. Maybe his mother-in-law had been right when she called Bob an anchor around Jane's neck. Maybe he was dragging the whole family under. Maybe they'll all drown because how can they be expected to keep their heads above water with him contributing nothing?

He's still crying and kicks the mop bucket. It doesn't tip over, only travels a few feet away.

He has to fight, he thinks. There's still time. But how? Maybe it's a choice to live your life tarred and feathered in fluorescent orange. Maybe Bob Coffen can shower it off.

▪ No matter how the room smells ▪

It's not long before the bandmates, sans Javier, clamber backstage, along with Kat and her kid. It appears as if Javier's threat had legs and he's flown the coop, leaving French Kiss no choice but to cancel the gig. The remaining members are incensed. They are speaking in terms of vengeance. It's Ace who spearheads these violent delusions. He advocates for immediate retribution and has been expressing these prerogatives via a manifesto on the high points of wanton carnage: "There will be justice," he filibusters while pacing, the rest of them forced to soak up his venom like bored sponges, "and I'm not talking about that judge-and-jury justice. Nothing civilized. Nope, there will be some extracurricular justice. Let's say that Acey isn't afraid to haunt the dark shadows of the law. I won't shy away from menace. It's in my blood. My granddaddy was a bootlegger, and his granddaddy was a bootlegger. I come from a lineage of those unafraid of an eclipse of conscience, if you know what I mean. I'll make sure Kathleen and me have an alibi. We'll go out of town for a weekend. We've been talking about Vegas or maybe something more relaxing. Catalina is supposed to be stunning. Who knows? It might be something as simple as the mud baths up in Calistoga. And while we're safely out of the area, Mr. Javier

Torres will be the victim of"—Ace uses air quotes for the next two words—"'random violence.' I won't rest until I'm wearing that bastard's Adam's apple like it's an ascot."

"Let's get bloody!" Bob says, using the signature line from Disemboweler IV as a way to commiserate with Ace.

"I knew I dug your style," Ace says and rubs Bob on the shoulder.

"It's only one show," Kat says. "I know you're disappointed, baby, but it's not your fault."

The other bandmates attempt to console Ace with low-grade clichés:

"We'll come back better than ever once we dial in a new bassist."

"We can be even greater than the great band we already are."

"French Kiss will climb higher on the throne of rock and roll."

"Tonight was supposed to be special!" Ace blurts, his voice getting really agitated. "I'd planned something really special and Mr. Javier Torres bastardized my special evening."

"You can't bastardize a time of day, bro," the French singer corrects again.

"I can't believe he did this to us," says Ace. "Tonight was going to be a really important night."

The room goes quiet.

Coffen is in a unique position to understand why Ace is so upset. Certainly, Kat's kid knows, too, but he doesn't seem to be locked into what's bothering Ace right now. Bob empathizes. He knows how deadly it can feel when you envision how something will play out, much like reading the signs at Björn's show: He and Jane were supposed to take in the information and use it as a way to better their marriage, but somehow Bob messed it up, made her so mad she walked out. Bob felt that sting so viscerally, watching Jane leave him in the ballroom, and he doesn't want Ace to endure something similar. He wants Ace to be saved from it. "Do it anyway," Bob says.

"What?"

"You know what," Coffen says. "Do it now."

"Do it backstage here?"

Bob nods and smiles. He's stopped crying. "Why not? Why wait one second longer?"

"Yeah?"

"Live a little," Coffen says.

Ace's eyes bounce between all present—the remaining members of French Kiss, Coffen, the boy, and finally, Kat. He fumbles through his pocket for something and kneels in front of her, still in his Kiss makeup and leather ensemble. "I meant to do this onstage in front of our legions of loyal fans. I wanted to make this something really special for you, my queen, but alas, there's nothing I can do about that now. And maybe it's better for Acey to do it like this. Because we'll never have a fancy life. Ours will be a modest existence. I'm not rich or famous and I never will be. I'm just a janitor."

"My dad has a better job than you," the boy says.

Ace only smiles at him and continues: "I'm another person getting by who's trying to do my best. But I've done hard living, which has taught me that when something makes you smile, that's what really matters. Like they say, life is short and life can be hard, but you and me, we make the world better for each other. I promise to always try to do that. I'll never quit trying to make you happy, and I'll always try to provide for you. I love your son."

"I'm not calling you dad," says the boy.

"Shhh," Kat says to him.

"Never call me dad, dude," Ace says. "But let's be friends, okay?"

The boy looks away.

"I love this band," Ace says. "I'm even starting to love my new friend, Bob. So here we all are in a room that stinks like puke, but that's the way the world is, right? No matter how happy you are, things are never ideal. There's always a catch. At least there always is for normal people. Maybe millionaires have it better. Who knows? But we're the normal people, and normal people make do with what the world gives them. We are happy no matter how the room smells."

"Oh, Ace," she says.

"I'm serious, my queen. No matter how the room smells we'll be happy. I know without any doubt that I want to spend the rest of my life with you. Let's go *mano a mano* versus the world together. I will love you and your son for all time. Will you make me the happiest Ace in the whole deck?"

"My dad's condo has a huge deck," the boy says.

"Stop it," Kat says to him. "This is what I want."

"What about what I want?" the boy asks.

"I hope you can be happy for me," she says. "I love you. Your dad loves you. Ace loves you. All of that makes you a lucky boy."

He doesn't say anything.

Kat looks at kneeling Ace, who says, "Will you please marry me before the rest of my hair falls out?"

"I can't wait to marry you."

He slides the ring on her finger.

He stands.

They smooch, hug each other.

To Bob, the boy sort of looks happy, whether he wants to or not.

French Kiss starts clapping and howling. Each member pushes in and hugs Ace and Kat and the boy.

There Bob Coffen is, humbled and alive and speechless. This is what he wants; this is what he needs—to answer his wife's dental bib. For if a motivating force is what she requires to swim against the sweeping, raging current of their complicated life, isn't the best thing Coffen can offer her what Ace has said to Kat: to be happy no matter how the room smells?

"Aren't you going to tell us congratulations, Bobby-boy?" Ace is asking.

"Can I hug, too?" Coffen asks.

"Get in here," Ace says.

Bob shuts his eyes and feels their bodies in his wide arms.

"We are happy as clams," Ace says.

"You got that right," Kat says.

"My man?" Ace says to the boy.

The kid nods—no small victory.

"Sorry you didn't get to gig tonight," Kat says to the whole band, but mostly to her newly anointed fiancé. "I know you were excited."

"It's more than fine," Ace says to her. "Especially since we might still be able to salvage the gig."

"How?" the French singer asks.

Ace looks at Coffen, all of them still tangled in a hug.

▪ Picking fights with sorcerers ▪

Who's to say that Javier actually needs to be Javier? The band only needs someone to stand there like a fool and pretend to play the bass, amp never getting turned on. They dress Coffen like an official member, make him up as an exact replica. He likes the face paint a lot. Then they mount the stage and Bob embarks upon his world premiere, a quasi-Javier, a bassist roaming the limelight.

When he first hits the stage, his feet begin to tingle, then his hands. His vision gets all spotty around the edges and Bob thinks he's going to pass out from nerves. He makes eye contact with Ace, who must see the panic in his eyes because, like a savvy veteran, he saunters over to Bob and says, "For the next forty-five minutes, we are rock gods." Coffen keeps his eyes shut for the whole first song, pretty much staying in one place, not getting into the performance too much. But when he hears the audience scream, when he hears all the heads present clap and whistle and hoot, Coffen opens his eyes and smiles.

Slowly, he test-drives the give in his hips.

By the time the set is half over, he whips his wig around in heavy metal spasms.

He waggles his tongue at pretty girls in the crowd and notices their welcoming flair as they flirt back with salacious gestures, one even baring her breasts for Coffen to appreciate.

Pelvic thrusts—à la Bob's pitch for Scroo Dat Pooch—haven't seemed so hopeless and clunky and arrhythmic in the history of rock and roll, but the music, the stage, the fancy lighting, all these aid his thrusts mightily.

He's getting even sweatier than he had been when riding the bike and he's having the time of his life. Feels wonderfully winded. Feels light-headed and loves every second of being live entertainment. Live! There's no computer screen. There's no streaming. No tape delay. No buffering. Bob Coffen is a human standing and sweating onstage in front of a roomful of other humans.

There's a surrender of sorts inside of Bob as he feels the hands of rock and roll all over him—as his adrenaline bucks. And if "surrender" is too strong a word, well, at least he's deciding something. Fuck his job. Fuck building one more game he doesn't believe in. Fuck security. Fuck steady paychecks if he hates the life he's secure in. Coffen is good at building games and if DG isn't satisfying him creatively, he can find another job. It might be the Kiss makeup, might be the javelin, could be the fact that he's been towing the line of his life and it isn't working. And right when French Kiss is in the middle of playing "Rock and Roll All Nite," Bob makes a decision onstage: This will be his fight song. Jane loves this one, too. Coffen closes his eyes and gets the tongue waggle working again, his hips doing an awful hula.

The set is a smash hit. They play two encores. Afterward, Ace says, "You saved our hind parts, Chump Change. If there's anything French Kiss can do to return the favor, you let us know."

"I need to win my wife back," Coffen says. "Will you guys help me?"

■ ■ ■

After the gig, there's nobody for Coffen to be with. His family is at home and his presence is forbidden. Ace and Kat have gone on their way. Schumann and Tilda—and unfortunately Björn—have peeled off in the SUV to who knows where. That leaves Bob all by his lonesome, back at the office after the concert. A man and his plock. He decides to take a page from Schumann's book, who found comfort and inspiration in putting on his old football uni. Coffen hasn't washed off his French Kiss makeup, hoping it will make him feel better, or at least a part of something, while he sits around the office.

This onstage surrender that Coffen felt while performing with French Kiss now jostles him into doing something sort of naughty with Scroo Dat Pooch. See, all he'd told Dumper and the rest of his team was that an avatar would run around town having sex with all these dogs, but he never said squat about who the avatar might be, who the avatar might be based on, who might be the inspiration for said avatar's likeness.

Bob, sitting at his desk in full French Kiss makeup, knows who shall have the starring role in Scroo Dat Pooch and continues coding with a renewed sense of adventure.

The plock strikes midnight.

Again.

Always.

It strikes twelve and Robert writes subversive code.

■ ■ ■

Noise. Noise at DG at what time? 4:00 AM? Coffen had passed out at his computer, head down on his desk, after making great headway on Scroo Dat Pooch.

The noise is music, and it's coming from a room nearby. LapLand—the place with the endless pools—also known as the place Ace liked to bathe while he squatted here. Coffen moseys over carefully, feeling as if he should have some kind of weapon in case there's an escaped convict or recently fired employee hunkered down to pluck off his old coworkers one by one with an automatic weapon. Bob picks up a stapler to defend himself, then puts it back down on the desk. Grabs a travel mug instead, takes a couple practice punches holding it, decides against this option, too. It's probably someone from the clean team getting an early start on his duties.

Bob pushes open the door and there's a young guy sitting in the lifeguard chair, listening to Johnny Cash.

"I thought you guys were only here during normal business hours," Bob says.

"We used to be. Starting today, Dumper put us on round-the-clock duty. Apparently, there was a lawsuit at a company in Copenhagen. An exec drowned swimming off-hours after drinking too much Aquavit."

"Do you think anybody will ever swim here at this hour?"

"Hope not."

"I feel like I'm having a dream right now and this is probably supposed to mean something symbolically."

"My name's Randy," the lifeguard says. "I have $50,000 worth of student loans and live with my mom. How could this be either of our dreams?"

Coffen brews some coffee in the kitchen and goes back to his desk, leaving Randy to his music and woes. Bob gets a text from Schumann: *Just came again.* ☺ *Tilda's incredible.*

Coffen: *What about your wife?*
She never understood the quarterback dormant inside me.
Little Schu?
Leave him out of this!
Where's Björn?
We let him go.
WTF!!??
Tilda thought it was the right thing to do.
This is bad, Coffen writes.
He promised not to hold any grudges.
You believed him?
I give people the benefit of the doubt.
He's going to kill us.
Tilda's horny. Ciao, Coffen!

■ ■ ■

The lack of grudge-holding from Björn doesn't last long. Forty-five minutes later, Björn is suddenly standing next to Coffen's desk. Björn is there holding a wee mouse by the tail. And the mouse happens to be wearing a wee football helmet and a wee lil' football uniform.

"How did you get in here?" Coffen asks.

"I'm holding this," Björn says, swinging the mouse some, "and your first question is how I got in here?"

"What's with the mouse?"

"Meet Schumann," says Björn.

"Give me a break."

"Here's the thing about picking fights with a sorcerer," Björn says. "Wouldn't you assume the sorcerer's coming out on top? And this guy didn't expect any consequences? What, he thought I'd simply let it go and shake his hand and buff his hubcaps and buy him a candied ham like all's forgiven? I'm not that mature. Ask my ex-wife. When I feel wronged, I fight dirty."

"What about Tilda?"

"She's fine. I might make her win the lottery. She's the one who convinced this maniac"—he points at wee swinging Schumann—"to let me go."

Schumann makes a series of some chirpy, peeping, mouse-type noises.

Björn shakes his head and says, "More lip service."

"You understand him?" Coffen asks.

"He keeps trying to apologize," Björn says, "as if there's an appropriate way to say sorry for violating my civil liberties and kneeing me in the testicles."

Bob takes a deep breath. He was caught off guard with Björn appearing out of thin air and waving the rodent around. But now Bob's pragmatism gets going: There is no such thing as magic. This is merely a mouse, a decoy, a dupe. Stay calm. Everything in life has a rational explanation.

Coffen's occupation lends itself to such a practical mind-set. In a sense, Bob is a magician when building a game—when he writes code, anything his imagination can dream up, he can make happen in the game. Say the character gets his foot run over by a magical lawn mower, and then the wound bleeds root beer dribbles from the toes, and if you drink the root beer you time-travel to Civil War–era Gettysburg. Nothing is impossible.

This, however, is real life and lots of things are impossible, so Bob says to Björn, "There's no way that mouse is Schumann."

"Call him if you don't believe me."

Coffen calls Schumann's cell. Björn continues to swing the mouse by the tail. The voicemail kicks in and there's a similar series of peeping mouse-type noises. Bob decides not to leave a message.

"That doesn't mean anything," Coffen says.

"You're a tough audience."

It dawns on Bob that the magician might be here to exact revenge on him, too. Not the mouse-type vengeance that Bob doesn't believe in, but the tried-and-true vengeance of alerting the proper authorities that Coffen was an accessory to the first kidnapping. "Björn," Bob starts pleading, nervously futzing with the plock's hands, changing the time to 5:15, then to 9:45, finally settling it back at midnight, "I didn't know what he was doing … I didn't ask him to kidnap you … I never put him up to this and actually tried to stop him from doing anything crazy. Please don't turn us over to the cops."

"I know, I know," he says. "We of the dark arts can look deep into a man's mind and appraise the truth. This isn't on you, which is why he's a mouse and you're still sitting there wearing some kind of clown makeup."

Bob can't tell Björn the truth, feels too stupid saying it out loud, but likes wearing the makeup because it reminds him of the action. They mounted the stage. The crowd cheered them on. Everybody was alive.

"Why are you here?" Bob asks Björn, now that it seems he's not about to fling any kind of terrible magical punishment Coffen's way.

"To say there are no hard feelings. And that I hope you and your wife still come to the show tonight."

"I'm trying to get her there. She's going for a world record tomorrow morning and her coach doesn't want her to go. But I'm currently hatching a master plan to win her back before the show. I'm getting a dental bib of my own soon. Say, do you have any dental bibs I can borrow?"

"Sure, in the trunk," he says.

"Thanks."

"Mostly I'm here to give you your rodent ally," Björn says, still holding Schumann up by his wee tail. "He's probably safer in your custody than mine."

Ethically, Coffen is supposed to say yes to this. But why on god's curdling earth would Bob want to be in charge of mousy Schumann? What if he loses him, squashes him, forgets to pay attention and a rogue kitty-cat enjoys an appetizer? Can Coffen handle any added pressure on his plate right now?

"Is he going to be like that forever?" asks Bob.

"Jury's still out."

"He has a wife and son."

"And the jury got kneed in the junk and thrown in the trunk. Hey, that rhymed."

Coffen sighs and sticks out his palm, and the magician places wee Schumann upon it to scamper. Bob thinks, *You are not Schumann, but on the slim chance you are, I don't want your disappearance on my conscience. I can board you for a bit. This might be good practice anyway, caring for an animal. Once I'm a weekend dad, I'll have to get some gloomy pet to keep me company. An iguana that sits in the corner on a log, barely ever moving, like me.*

It compels Bob to blurt, "I really need that dental bib."

"Then let's get you one," Björn says.

▪ Student of the ocean ▪

"One more peep and you're going in the glove box," Coffen says to Schumann, who will not shut up with his squeaks. Björn's given Bob a dental bib and now Coffen sits in his car, contemplating what to write on it. Or trying to contemplate, if the damn mouse would shut up.

Bob's threat seems to work because the rodent immediately goes silent.

Is that contrition in his beady eyes? He sulks on Bob's shoulder, minding his manners, a furry little gentleman.

Nobody wants to be in a box, Coffen thinks. *Not even a mouse.*

It's hot in Bob's car. He can smell the sautéing-cabbage funk from his armpits. And the mouse, he reasons, is probably producing his own stench.

A meteorologist might call the barometric pressure *unseasonably high.*

Coffen texts his daughter: *Wanna see real life sea horses at aquarium today?*

Coffen texts his son: *Sea horses at aquarium today?*

Margot: *How long will it take?*

Coffen: *Only a couple hours. There's fro-yo in it for you.*

Margot: *No thanks*

Then Brent's response comes in: *i'm gaming*

Bob: *Please?*
Brent: *fine*
Pick you up in 20?
fine

And off Coffen and Schumann zoom. He places the mouse in the glove box, says, "It's best if my family doesn't see you."

The mouse squeaks and peeps his counterargument, but to no avail.

Bob figures it's also wise to wipe the Kiss makeup off his face before he has to explain it to the kids. He doesn't want to say goodbye to it, but he can always ask Ace to reapply it later.

Coffen calls Jane on the way, wanting to warn her of his impending arrival at the home he's verboten from, but it's Erma who answers Jane's cell with, "What?"

"I'm coming by to pick up Brent."

"We already know."

"Has Jane said anything about the show I invited her to tonight?"

"We think it's an unnecessary distraction the night before she goes for the record."

"What does she think?"

"We're concerned that any unnecessary stimuli the night before could clutter her psyche, like garbage in the ocean."

"That sounds like Gotthorm."

"He's brilliant."

"Does Jane want to come with me tonight?"

Erma, talking to somebody, presumably Jane, yells, "He's asking questions about the magic show."

"She has the tickets I left with Gotthorm, right?" Bob asks.

"Yeah, yeah, we've got the tickets stuck to the fridge."

"Can I quickly talk to Jane? For like ten seconds?"

"He wants to talk to you for like ten seconds."

Coffen can't make out Jane's voice in the background, but soon Erma says, "Honk when you're here and Brent will come out."

Erma hangs up.

Coffen honks when he's there for Brent to come out.

But it's not his son who exits first. "Hi, Dad," Margot says. "Are you sure you guys aren't getting divorced?"

"I'll be home after your mom breaks the record."

"G-Ma is packing up a lot of your stuff."

"Don't worry about G-Ma. Only worry about your mom and me."

"Isn't that what I'm doing?"

"Why don't you want to come to the aquarium today?"

"I've been in the ocean all week."

"Please?" asks Bob.

"Fine. Let me go get my iPad."

"Leave it. Come on. Let's go have some fun."

"I need my iPad."

Bob can make this concession, so long as she comes along. "Fine, go get it."

Margot walks inside the house, and Bob hears some scratching noises coming from inside the glove compartment. Some of Schumann's past peeping was obviously negative, yet these scratches sound supportive to Coffen, somehow optimistic, as though each rake of unruly rodent nail says, *Way to play it, Bob. I think you're on the right road.*

"I have to be home by 2:30," Margot says, walking back up to the car. "Ro and I are going to ancient Greece."

Coffen has to be done by about that time, too, so he can go prepare for his big plan, his way of luring Jane to come with him to the show, with the help of French Kiss. "We'll have you home in plenty of time to travel the world. Here comes your brother."

■ ■ ■

The aquarium is on the outskirts of their suburb, bleeding into the adjacent one. If kids still liked going outside their rooms to play, this part of town would be immensely popular. There's a bowling alley, a roller-skating rink, and of course the aquarium. But these escapisms aren't in vogue.

Coffen had actually been surprised that the aquarium was still in business when Schumann mentioned it. Judging from the empty parking lot, he's not alone.

In fact, to say that the sea horse exhibit is exhibiting a sparse public interest would be a vulgar euphemism. The aquarium is empty. Only the Coffens and a few straggling employees. Why would nobody come and bask in the unmitigated splendor of these underwater steeds? Anybody's guess.

But the silver lining in this sea horse cloud is that Coffen, Margot, and Brent can easily view each aquarium. There are sixteen small ones, all in the middle of the room and shaped like little domes with varying species of sea horse. The nice thing about the size and shape of the individual orbs is that they allow a 360-degree view of the horses' habitats—Margot and Brent rotate all the way around the tiny universes, following the creatures as they slalom about. Some of the sea horses are the size of coffee beans, while others stretch out six, maybe seven inches. There's a wide array of colors and patterns on their bodies, but they all have those thin, elongated noses.

Coffen stands next to his daughter, watching the sea horses. "Is it better than seeing them online?" Bob asks her.

"It's different. I don't know if it's better or not."

"They are beautiful in person, aren't they?"

"I can zoom in and get closer to them when me and Ro go swimming."

"Right, but here you can actually appreciate their uniqueness. There are living, breathing sea horses contained in this environment."

"Right, but if I zoom in I can really analyze that uniqueness."

"Right, but seeing them here gives you a sense of scale."

"Right, but if I swim up quietly, I can hold one in my hand."

"Right, but that isn't your real hand."

"Right, but it serves the same purpose. There's a fish in my hand that I'll probably never get to see in the wild."

"You should learn to scuba," Bob says, hoping to find Margot a real-world hobby. "I'll happily pay for those classes."

"Maybe."

Now there's an employee's voice calling, "Hey! Hey!" and waving at the three Coffens. "This one's about to give birth. Get over fast and observe science firsthand."

They make their way to the aquarium in question.

"How do you know?" Coffen asks the woman.

"Because I'm a college-degreed scientist is how," she says.

The particular sea horse in question is in the dome alone. It is bright orange, almost fluorescent orange, or that's the association Bob makes. It's near the bottom of the tank and has wrapped its tail around a rock to steady itself. A hole has opened in the abdomen. Its body lunges in staccato, contracting motions.

"She's going to be a mommy?" Brent says to the crabby scientist.

But it's Margot who answers: "A daddy. With sea horses, the daddies give birth to the babies."

"Aren't you a smart girl?" the scientist says.

"I spend a lot of time under the sea."

"Good for you."

"She means under the sea on the computer," Coffen says.

The scientist smiles at Margot. "You're smart to take advantage of every resource to learn more about nature."

At that, there's the first volley of newborns flying out of the hole; somewhere between twenty and thirty tiny sea horses shoot out, rolling in the water. They are pale, wiggling, the size of slivers of fingernail. Once birthed, they swim haphazardly, directionless.

Margot pulls out her iPad and starts shooting video.

"Enjoy the moment," Bob says.

"I am."

"Just be here."

"I am."

Another large burst of brand-new sea horses dash from the abdomen.

"Just exist in the here and now," he says to her, knowing that she's not going to hear him, that she's incapable of listening to any of his words. What she doesn't understand is that they're warnings.

"I am here. I am now," Margot says.

More babies tumble from the father.

"Does the daddy feed them all?" Brent asks Bob.

But that doesn't stop a certain scientist from piping up. "They aren't like people. The daddies don't care for the babies once they're born."

"Who does?"

"They have to take care of themselves," Margot says, continuing to film it all.

"You are a fantastic student of the ocean," the scientist says to her.

"Thanks for noticing."

"It's scary that nobody takes care of them," Brent says, looking up at Coffen. "Don't you think that's scary?"

"Yes, it's scary," Bob says, "but you're safe. Don't worry."

Everybody is staring into the aquarium. They are transfixed. Coffen can't comprehend why he ever felt so seduced by artifice. What was so enthralling about the unreal? Why had he stationed himself away from the present? What could have ever seemed more compelling about fake lives when all this life was happening around him?

"Isn't it incredible to witness stuff like this?" the scientist says.

Every Coffen nods, spellbound.

▪ Scout'sHonor!® ▪

Tilda isn't buying the story Coffen stammers through. He'd hoped that she'd kind of accept the fact that the quarterback-clad mouse he now swings slowly by its tail before her eyes is Schumann. Unfortunately, she's proving impervious to the spell of his spiel.

This is transpiring at Taco Shed in the late afternoon—after fro-yo, after Bob had dropped his children off at home. Tilda mans the register. As this is the chain's pre-dinner lull, no other customers or employees are there. Her muscles seem especially plump on this fine day, in that fine uniform.

Her eyes stay trained on the dangling mouse. "I didn't know there were any other ways men could break up with me; I thought I'd seen it all before, but now you're trying to tell me an evil magician turned him into a mouse."

"He's not an evil magician per se," Coffen says. "Honestly, his motives remain pretty obtuse to me. But I wouldn't say outright evil."

"I knew Schumann was married and that our affair, no matter how torrid, had a short shelf life, but now you're waving a mouse in my face saying that's him? Jesus, I didn't think it would get any worse than when that welder gave me gonorrhea on Valentine's Day."

Coffen continues to swing Schumann back and forth by the tail like he's trying to hypnotize her. "Tilda, I wouldn't make this up. Frankly, my imagination isn't capable of making something like this up."

"I thought me and you were friends."

"We are."

"Then why are you lying to me?"

Bob Coffen is not the man for the job of mouse-sitting right now. Normally, sure, he'd be happy to place Schumann in a shoebox with some handfuls of newly shorn grass, a wedge of fine Danish cheese for him to nibble the day away, an exercise wheel to burn off those heavy dairy calories. But not tonight. Tonight has to be all about Jane and the show with no distractions.

"I was hoping you'd baby-sit him," Coffen says to Tilda.

"What now?"

"Will you watch him for a few hours?"

"Baby-sit the mouse?"

"Please."

"You make that welder who gave me the drip seem like the most romantic man in the universe."

"Between you and me, I'm about to go try and win my wife back. I can't be responsible for Schumann tonight."

"Maybe that welder's number is still listed. Gonorrhea really isn't that big of a deal when you think about it in context with all the other atrocities going on in the world today—a little gonorrhea, big whoop . . ."

There are certain sentences that human beings are never prepared to utter until they leave the lips, and here goes a doozy from Bob: "I would never say this mouse was Schumann unless this mouse was indeed the notorious Schumann."

"No wonder my daughter lives in a car with a bun in the oven. No wonder she loves that loser. Look at the example I set. Jesus, will you stop swinging him by his tail?"

Bob stops swinging him by his tail, stows him on his shoulder once more.

"On the off chance I did screw that mouse last night, treat him with a little respect, will ya?"

Now Schumann pipes up a bit on his own behalf, squeaking and peeping. Both humans look at the wee quarterback. Tilda even nods a couple times as though she understands his rodent dialect.

"Maybe that is Reasons with His Fists," she says, "but either way, this is a restaurant, and I can't harbor a rodent here. If the health department found out, I'd lose my job. You're on your own."

"I understand," Coffen says, not understanding at all— wait a hot damn sec: She runs an intercom-sex operation out of this joint but is worried about boarding a mouse for a few hours?

"Did he say anything nice about me?" Tilda asks.

"What?"

"I'm not saying he is a mouse. But for the sake of argument, before he got turned into that thing, did he say any nice stuff?"

"Tilda, he raved about you."

She smiled. "Thanks. I don't even care if you're lying. Would you like a Mexican lasagna for the road?"

"I'd love one."

She disappears into the back for a couple minutes, comes back out with it. "Will you eat it here?"

"I have to run."

"Stay a couple more minutes and eat. It's the least you

can do after waving that mouse around and telling me I took it to bed."

They make small talk, bicker some, stay away from any more direct discussions about wee Schumann shelved on Bob's shoulder. It only takes about six bites to choke down the Mexican lasagna. Coffen should chew more when he eats. If he doesn't want to do it for his digestive tract, then he should do it for anybody forced to watch the splattering pageantry in person.

Then he and Schumann walk out front to depart Da Taco Shed.

Coffen barely has time to unlock his car when Tilda throws the restaurant's door open and comes tearing into the parking lot after him, screaming, "I need to ask you a couple questions, Bob."

"Of course."

"Is that mouse on your shoulder my lover, Reasons with His Fists, a.k.a. your neighbor, Schumann?"

"Why are you asking me that?"

"Please answer the question."

"I don't understand."

"Tell me."

Coffen nods. "Yes, I think this mouse is maybe Schumann."

Tilda stares at Coffen's face. She's staring at his face in such a way it's making him really uncomfortable.

"What are you doing?" he asks, growing more alarmed with every second of her measured appraisal.

"Watching your nose."

"Why?"

"For blood."

"Why would I have a bloody nose?"

"I chopped up a Scout'sHonor!® and laced your Mexican lasagna."

"What's Scout'sHonor!®?" Coffen asks.

"It's a pill. An over-the-counter truth serum."

"That's a real thing?"

"Tell a lie while you're on it," Tilda says, "and a pond of blood will rip-roar from your nose."

"How long has that been on the market?"

"Let's stay focused on the questions about Schumann."

"Is it FDA-approved?"

"If you don't wanna tell me the truth from your mouth, your nose will tell me what I need to know," says Tilda.

"Why'd you lace my lasagna?"

"I have to know the truth. So please say it once more: Is that mouse really my lover, Reasons with His Fists, a.k.a. your neighbor, Schumann?"

Bob doesn't know how to answer that. His head says no, of course not. His heart says, I doubt it but it is the tiniest bit conceivable, after Bob saw Björn morph the ballroom floor into ice baths. In a sense it doesn't matter what he thinks about the likelihood of Schumann's mouse status. It's up to Scout'sHonor!®.

Bob decides to go with his heart: "Yeah, I'm pretty sure the mouse is Schumann."

"I need a definitive answer."

"It's him."

She ogles Bob's nose, which stays bone dry. Tilda looks surprised. So does Coffen. Then once she's convinced that there's nary a deception on the premises, Tilda says, "Now that I know for certain you're not lying, I'm happy to baby-sit."

"Maybe the truth serum doesn't work," says Bob.

"I don't know if I can believe your story, and I certainly don't believe that hustling magician. But I've used Scout'sHonor!® many times on many men and I know that it works like a charm.

"Life is getting weirder," she says, taking the mouse from Bob, holding her palms flat so Schumann can nose around, walk in little circles, tickle with his whiskers. She brings him up close to her face and makes smooching noises. He responds with squeaks that seem jubilant.

Then she holds him right up to her left eye: "My god, it might really be him."

"It's a lot to stomach, I know."

"Sorry for dosing you."

"I understand why."

"You're a good friend," says Tilda.

"So are you."

"And our list keeps getting longer."

"Our list?"

"Cops, monsters, prudes, and mice," she says, still eyeballing Schumann.

■ The Coffen front lawn ■

Bob, his new dental bib, and French Kiss are all in the band's van, driving to Coffen's house. It's time to launch OPERATION WIN BACK JANE.

The band members are all in full French Kiss makeup.

Bob is wearing a new black suit. He's going all-in to get Jane to come along to Björn's show tonight.

His secret weapon, at least from Coffen's own perspective, is the dental bib. He's been lamenting what to write on it, deciding only a matter of minutes ago to write their names on it: JANE, MARGOT, BRENT.

If Jane needs a reason to keep trying, won't this bib be the perfect answer for her? Obscenely bigheaded over his bib idea, he shows it to Ace. They are in the back of the van with all the gear. The French singer drives. The drummer rides shotgun.

"What do you think?" Bob says, fluttering the bib with pride.

"Meh," Ace says.

"What do you mean 'meh'?"

"It's pretty sentimental."

"This is the exact time to be sentimental. This is the life and death of my family."

"Listen, I'm only one man," says Ace. "I'm only one

mortal man named Ace commenting on this dental bib, but I don't think it's the way to go."

"If there's ever a time to go sentimental, it's tonight."

"I'm only one mortal balding man named Ace, but I think you can do better."

"Turn right up here?" the singer says.

"Yeah, right, then second left," Bob says.

"Check."

"I'm with Ace," the drummer says, "don't be so sappy."

"You guys, I have to convince her to come along to the show. She's not going to want to come and I have to make her."

"Why won't she want to come?" Ace says.

"She's trying to break the world record for treading water starting tomorrow morning. Her coach says she shouldn't go anywhere tonight, needs her rest."

"The coach is right, dude," the drummer says. "She needs to be well rested and hydrated."

"Of course," Coffen says, "but she'll still get plenty of rest. The show is only from 7:30 to 9:00. We'll have her in bed by 10:00 PM."

"Chump Change, I'm on your side," Ace says. "No doubt, you're my dog in this race. We're on our way to try and help you, remember that. But I have to ask: Are you doing the right thing? Shouldn't you be in favor of her doing everything she can to prepare for the race, even if that means skipping this magic thingie?"

"She's probably not even going to break the record," Bob says.

"Whoa, that's fucked," the French singer says.

"That's disgustingly fucked," the drummer says.

"I gave up cussing," says Ace, "but allow me to weigh in with Pig Latin: That's *uck-fayed.*"

"It's not *uck-fayed*," Bob says.

"Dude, it's totally *uck-fayed*," the drummer says.

"I'm not being mean," Coffen says. "I'm only saying she's tried and failed at breaking this record four times already. We have to be realistic."

"Dude, do you think she can break the record or not?" the drummer says.

"That's not important," Bob says.

"It's pretty important," says Ace. "Do you?"

"Of course I think she can break it." The Scout'sHonor!® racing through Coffen's bloodstream goes to work, its formula producing the promised results. Bob has lied. Now his nose starts bleeding.

"Did you do some blow or something?" Ace asks.

Coffen wipes his nose on the back of his hand. "No, it's nothing."

"That's not nothing." Ace asks the drummer to see if there are any leftover fast food napkins in the glove compartment. Luckily, there are. Bob holds a bundle up to his face.

"Am I a rock star, Chump Change?" says Ace.

"I don't understand the question," Coffen says.

"Am I a millionaire rock star playing concerts at sold-out arenas around the globe?"

"Is this the left I take?" the singer says.

"Yes," Bob says.

"Then what after that?"

"Then your third right into my subdivision."

"Got it."

Coffen says to Ace, "You aren't a rock star."

"Exactly right I'm not a rock star. But I am one to Kathleen. She comes to every gig I play. She loves me. She

FIGHT SONG ■ 191

cheers like crazy. She believes in me, no matter what. Do you believe in Jane like that?"

"Of course I . . ." Bob trails off. He feels the faucet in his nose open up a bit more, the blood coming at a faster rate. Wow, had he not known this before? Was he aware of the fact he didn't think Jane could break the record? It makes him feel like complete shit, this idea that he doubted her chances. Because Ace is right: He should be more like Kat; he should believe in Jane's talent and skill and practiced abilities. He should believe that she can do anything she puts her mind to.

And it's occurring to Bob that they're also right about this evening's itinerary. He is being *uck-fayed*. He is being selfish. He should not be asking Jane to go to Björn's show. He should be encouraging her. He should be doing everything in his power to make sure she succeeds at everything that's important to her.

"You guys are right," Coffen says. "Let's make a couple changes to what we're going to do once we get to my house." He turns the bib over, writes something else on the back of it, and fastens the sign around his neck.

Ace reads it and smiles.

■ ■ ■

Early evening, the sun creeps down the horizon. Coffen's wife, two children, and Erma all stand on the front steps of the light gray house, summoned by Bob and his cohorts: the dulcet stylings of French Kiss, sans Javier Torres, of course, who's moved onto greener pastures, ones where all passersby are no doubt awestruck by his sonic chops. The three remaining members—in full French Kiss makeup— serenade Coffen's entire family.

Coffen had knocked on the front door once the band was all set up on the lawn. Margot opened the door and asked what was going on. Bob said, "Go get the whole family." For once she did as she was told without making a big stink about not knowing why—or maybe she did know why and was rooting for Bob. Yes, he likes that idea quite a bit.

So:

See the whole Coffen clan congregated on the porch. Ace strums away on an acoustic guitar. The drummer keeps the beat on a snare drum that's propped up on a stand in front of him. The French singer sings a yarn from the vault of the Kiss catalog, perhaps their most renowned ditty, "Rock and Roll All Nite." They've done some progressive rearranging of the song's components and currently, even though the rendition is only beginning, they are already playing the chorus, albeit a slower, jazzier, more romantic lilt than the original band ever intended.

Coffen wears his reconceived dental bib around his neck. On it is the following message: GOOD LUCK TOMORROW, JANE!

His family claps for French Kiss as the song ends.

Then Ace starts talking, "Thanks very much; you are too kind. Thank you. Wow. What a fantastic response. We're really happy to be here playing the Coffen front lawn tonight."

"Who are these guys?" Margot asks Coffen.

"My band."

"Your band?" she says.

"Your band?" Jane says.

"Your band?" the band echoes.

"Let's not get ahead of ourselves, Chump Change," Ace says. "We're not your band exactly."

"I thought the gig went well," Coffen says. "I want to learn bass and play with you guys. I'll give my all and promise to practice night and day."

"How about some beginner's lessons and we'll see how it goes?" Ace says. "We'll start there."

"So I'm in the band?" Coffen asks.

"No," says Ace, "but you can consider yourself on a temporary French Kiss scholarship while we figure out the lineup situation. We won't turn on your amp, but you'll wear the signature look and work the signature moves. You'll be our temp until we iron things out and who knows, if you prove to be a savant on your instrument, maybe you will find yourself a permanent addition to our lineup. That good enough for now?"

Bob nods, looks each member of the band in the eyes, and thanks them. He hadn't expected to ask to be anything more than a onetime replacement, but it feels good to hear they'd consider him as a permanent member should he learn the bass inside and out. Now the onus is on Coffen. Do the work. Practice. And see what happens.

"I'm not totally sure what's going on out here," Jane says.

"Gotthorm wouldn't like this," Erma says.

"What's going on," Bob says, "is that I'm here to apologize to you, Jane. I'm here to say that I should never have suggested we go to Björn's show tonight. I'm here because I love you and I love our children and I know you're going to break the world record on this attempt."

"You think I'm going to do it this time?" she asks.

"I really do. Get all the rest you need. Break that record. And we'll talk after you're the world champion." Coffen grips the crumpled and bloodied napkins in his pocket, in case he needs to retrieve them to swipe at a bleeding nose, but not one drip falls from his nose. "Now can we get back to enjoying the music?" Bob asks.

Jane smiles, nods, stares at him.

"Yeah!" says Brent.

Even Margot, who's got her iPad out to record all this, says, "Let's hear another one."

Ace laughs and says, "We love the enthusiasm we're seeing from the crowd on the Coffen front lawn! Music is about the fans, and we love each and every one of you. You never know what to expect at a new venue, but the Coffen front lawn is winning a huge place in our hearts!"

The four Coffens all clap.

Erma stands with her hands on her hips.

Hopefully, no soulless spies from the HOA observe this unauthorized performance or they'll no doubt pop off a belligerent email to Bob, a threat cluttered with propaganda and rhetorical questions—*shouldn't the music being broadcast within our subdivision's collective earshot represent the tastes of all the residents rather than a mere few? Isn't every one of our ears entitled to tones that tickle its tastes?*

"Excuse me," Jane says. "Will you play 'Rock and Roll All Nite' again? That's one of my favorites."

"Your taste in rock and roll is rock solid," Ace says.

French Kiss strikes up the song again.

Bob pats his bib and says to Jane, "Good luck."

▪ Shame-cave ▪

If one thing is utterly obvious to Coffen once he leaves his family for the night and goes back to DG, it is he has to stop lying to himself. What an oddly timed revelation earlier in French Kiss's van, realizing consciously for the first time that he didn't really support his wife. And that makes him wonder what else he doesn't know. He's still dosed on Scout'sHonor!® so he walks toward the bathroom to ogle his face in the mirror while he finds out about himself, one nosebleed at a time.

On his way there, however, he hears more Johnny Cash coming from LapLand. He opens the door and walks in. There the lifeguard sits, perched high in his chair, guarding an empty pool.

"Oh, fantastic, it's the guy who thinks this is all a dream."

"I now know this is real," Coffen says.

"I'm pretty busy, so do you mind?"

"Will you play a game with me?"

"No thanks," the lifeguard says.

"Is my nose bleeding?"

"Is that part of the game? Because I'm pretty sure I said that I didn't want to play."

"Is my nose bleeding?"

"You're going to keep badgering me until I answer you, right?"

"Yes."

"Your nose is not bleeding."

"I love my wife and I believe in her," Bob says.

"Okay."

"Is my nose bleeding?"

"Nope."

"I love my kids and I believe in them, too."

Bob pauses, shrugs.

"Still no blood," the lifeguard says.

"I love my job," Bob says, not even needing to ask about his nose this time because he feels it rupture. The blood gushes and Coffen doesn't even wipe it, lets it soak the front of his new suit. "I have to quit this job."

"You and me both," the lifeguard says. "You give me the creeps."

"I've worked here for ten years."

"You poor son of a bitch."

"How do you make any big changes to your life once you have all these responsibilities?" Bob asks, although he's turning to walk out without giving the lifeguard any time to answer.

■ ■ ■

Bob hadn't expected any additional hours to work on Scroo Dat Pooch, but with an empty Sunday night, why not polish this turd to an incredible sheen? The code he writes makes the game look better, graphics getting downright good, and the better it looks—he reasons—the greater the opportunity for tomorrow morning's status meeting to be an incredible unveiling, a self-sabotage of extraordinary measures.

"What time is it, Robert?" he says to himself.

"The plock strikes twelve, Robert."

"Does it, Robert my boy?"

"Indeed, it does, Robert."

■ ■ ■

Coffen codes away and his phone rings about an hour later. "Bob is me," he says.

"Somebody gives you a gift of free tickets and you spit in his fucking face of generosity?" a voice says, slurring his words dramatically.

"Björn?"

"I turned your colleague into a rodent, Bob. If I didn't know better, I'd think you were antagonizing me by flaking on my show. I'm a big deal, man. I'm famous. I have over three thousand fans on Facebook. I'm a true miracle worker and you spit in the face of me and my show's free tickets? Nobody treats me like I'm some walking colostomy bag and gets away with it. I mean, I have a statue of myself in my backyard."

"Are you drunk?"

"Oh, sure, oh, yeah, my wife sought the solace she needed in the arms of another man and also two women she met in hotel bars because I failed to satisfy her sexually. But also she failed me in the realm of communication, right? I never knew that she wasn't sexually satisfied or I would have done something about it. I am a sorcerer. I could have made her clit grow to the size of a pie tin. I could have pleased her in ways she's never even pondered, but again, I didn't know there was a problem. The point is that the communication broke down. And now, me and you, our communication is faltering. I give you free tickets. I excuse your kidnapping. I wipe the slate clean. And you can't even live up to your end of the agreement and come to the show?"

"So you're wasted," Coffen says.

"I'm so drunk that it should be called something else. I'm 'floff-mongered.' Float that new bit of slang around and see if it catches on."

"Where are you anyway?"

"I'm in my shame-cave."

"Your what?"

"This place I go when I need to be alone with my self-sympathy," he says. "When my floff-mongering is front and center."

"What's wrong?"

"Tonight's show was a disaster. I had to flee the scene as a fugitive. I could have used a friendly face in the audience, Bob. Shit went terribly wrong. It was a new illusion. I made everybody's chair fly about fifteen feet in the air. I told them to hold on tight. I told them there was no real danger. As long as they stayed steadied, they'd only be floating there, say, thirty seconds or so before I let them back down. But then one woman puked. Then another did. And that made them all wobbly and woozy and soon one fell off and then another and pretty soon everyone was falling from the sky and landing on the carpet in screaming heaps. I kept saying to them, 'You are safe, but you are vulnerable. That's the balancing act. That's what the flying-chair metaphor represents.' But it was too late. They were already starting to fall."

"Did anyone get hurt?"

"Lots of them got hurt," Björn says.

"And you left?"

"Hell yeah, I left. It was a bloodbath. I split out the fire exit once they all started plummeting."

"I'm glad we weren't there, or Jane and I would have fallen, too."

"Or maybe it would have gone as expected had you been there to cheer me on, man. Even magicians need friends."

"Are you blaming me?"

"I think so, yeah."

"How does that make any sense?"

Bob hears a noise on Björn's end of the phone that sounds like a can opening, then a desperate sip being taken: "In my mind's eye," Björn says, "the floating-chair illusion made perfect sense. Everyone would sit, perched high and mighty, and I'd give an inspiring speech about the travails of monogamy, learning to balance all the chaos and unpredictability of life. But once the first lady fell, it was a total shit show."

"What did you think was going to happen?"

"I thought maybe two or three people would fall, total. Gotta crack a couple eggs to make an omelet, as the kids say. Now I need to get out of this town ASAP."

"Not too ASAP," Coffen says. "You have to turn Schumann back."

"Oh, do I have to turn back your mousy associate?" he yells. "Is that what Björn has to do?"

"Can we meet first thing tomorrow—me, you, and Schumann? Please? Let's talk about our options."

"I haven't totally decided whether I even want to turn him back. He kidnapped me. Let's not forget that piece of the puzzle."

"Well, that's what we should talk about. Let me plead his case to you."

"Fine, plead his case. Now I need to focus on my shame-cave. I need to sulk. Need to . . . Wait, what's my new slang again?"

"Floff-monger."

"Yes, I need some serious floff-mongering."

Björn hangs up and Bob ponders magic. At first, it had seemed so clear that Schumann was not the mouse, but the longer this is going on, Coffen actually wants it to be true—wants to believe in Björn's powers. Why not? Bob writes code, breathes code. He lives like a character in the worst video game of all time: slowly fizzling out, level by level, until there's nothing left except a pile of fluorescent orange that needs to be swept up. If there's some magic out there that can help him avoid the dust pan, well, it sure sounds good right about now.

▪ What's wrong with a mouse man? ▪

When last Coffen reviewed the hallowed tenets of baby-sitting, it was his understanding that the custody of said baby in the said sitter's stead was a temporary arrangement. As in, thanks, Tilda, for taking wee mousy Schumann off Coffen's hands for a few hours, but he's now come to reclaim the great rodent booty that is Bob's neighbor.

However, a certain Taco Shed employee doesn't want to cough him up.

"His family gets home soon," Coffen says to Tilda, standing in the doorway of her apartment early the following morning and hoping that this idea contains the cocktail of persuasion. "We've got to get him back to his life."

It's approximately 6:30 AM on Monday morning. The mouse runs around Tilda's cupped hands. "I think he's happy. We were up all night together; we bonded in a very spiritual way. He has a look in his eyes that tells me he'd like to stay like this forever. Honestly, this might be the kind of change that he truly wanted."

"Can I please have him back?"

"He might be the perfect man for me," Tilda says.

"He's not a man."

"Sure he is, but he's also so small he can't hurt me, and that's what I've always wanted."

Schumann makes some chirpy, mousy noises and is clearly shaking his wee head to the contrary of her statements.

"He has a wife and kid," Coffen says.

"He told me all about them way back when he first started being one of my intercom clients. And he told me a lot after we did it in the SUV. Honestly, I don't think he'd miss too much sleep over never seeing them again."

"He's a good father."

"But maybe he'd make a better mouse, at least for the foreseeable future, and trust me: I'll take incredible care of him."

"I don't doubt it."

"He's the perfect pet," she says.

Coffen wants to say something supportive, something about how extraordinary she is and that she deserves a partner of the same species. Sure, she's had a stable of bad relationships. Yes, life can be hard. No, she's not perfect. But she can't wrap her heart in muscles, like a fragile trinket in bubble wrap and stop trying to find somebody who might make her happy. Those are all the things Coffen hopes to convey, and it comes out like this: "You don't need a mouse man, Tilda."

"What's wrong with a mouse man?"

"How will you two ever dance together?"

"That's a sacrifice I'm willing to make."

"You deserve a full-blown human being."

"Not sure I want one of those."

Schumann now stands solely on his hind legs and is shaking his wee head.

"But look at how he's shaking his head," Coffen offers up.

"His head's not moving."

"I can see him shaking it."

"I don't think so."

"Look at him."

"That's an optical illusion," says Tilda.

"What is?"

"His head shaking."

"I thought you said he wasn't even moving his head!"

"Damn," she says. "Entrapped again. You got me." She hands Schumann over to Bob, placing him in his flattened palms. Schumann gives a creepy wee mousy smile and scampers up to perch on Coffen's shoulder. He smells like something . . . jasmine? Coffen sniffs Schumann several times.

"I doused him in lavender body oil," Tilda says. "Honestly, the natural smell was wretched."

"Makes sense, I guess."

"The magician turning him back?" she asks.

"Supposedly. We're meeting this morning."

"Can I come? I've never seen real magic before."

"I'm not sure he'd appreciate me bringing you along."

"Only one way to know for sure."

"I shouldn't."

"Call him and ask," she says.

Coffen caves in and calls.

"Are you seriously asking me that?" Björn says. "My hangover's no joke."

"I am unfortunately asking you that, yes."

"My god, Coffen, you are high-maintenance."

"Can she come?"

"I haven't even decided that I'm going to turn him back."

"I'm sure he's learned his lesson," Coffen says.

"How are you sure of that?"

"Tell him we can meet at Taco Shed and I'll throw in a round of breakfast Mexican lasagnas on the house," says Tilda. "As many as he can eat."

Coffen relays the offer, and the magician says, "I agree to the proposed terms. See you in twenty."

■ ■ ■

In twenty, Coffen, Tilda, and Schumann stand face-to-face with Björn. Bob introduces her to the magician, who's wearing sunglasses; his moustache is smashed and he stinks like booze.

"Looks like you had a long night of floff-mongering," says Bob.

"It was pure madness."

"Can I make you boys breakfast?" Tilda asks, and all parties seem extremely interested in that prospect. She unlocks the place, tells them no other employees will be there for an hour, when they begin to prep for the 8:00 AM rush. Everyone lingers around the register while she prepares the breakfast Mexican lasagnas. Schumann still sits on Coffen's shoulder.

"Why should I do him any favors?" Björn says, not taking off his sunglasses. "He kidnapped me."

"You'd be doing me a favor," Coffen says. "And his family. Please?"

"Chow time," suggests Tilda, holding a whole tray of breakfast Mexican lasagnas that are actually completely identical in structure to regular non-breakfast Mexican lasagnas. Soon, they're all gorging on grease.

Tilda speaks up first: "Maybe Björn is right. I mean, Schumann did kidnap him, which if memory serves correctly is a felony. This seems like it might be an appropriate punishment given the severity of the crime."

Schumann shakes his wee head very much to the contrary again.

"I'm sure," Coffen says to Tilda, "if he stays a mouse you'd be happy to watch over him as a kind of gentle guardian, is that right? Is that how you'd like to see this end—you get your pet and his son grows up without a father?"

"I'd be open to that suggestion," she says.

"We're talking about a husband and a father and he needs to be human once more," Coffen says.

"I grew up without a father," Tilda says, "and I'm fine."

"Me, too," the magician chimes in.

Bob sighs. "Me, too."

Björn unwraps another Mexican lasagna, enjoys a bite, and says, "You know what? After last night's awful show, I want to get out of this godforsaken town and forget all about it. I don't want to have this guy on my conscience for the rest of my life. I don't need that. Believe me, there's enough on my conscience. You don't think I retaliated dark-arts-style once the ink dried on our divorce papers? You bet I did. I'm not proud of it, but I got the last laugh. Was what I did to her childish and vindictive? No doubt. I am regretful. Yes, there is shame in my shame-cave. So I don't need to add to it for no real reason." Then he puts his finger right in Schumann's wee face. "But snap out of this quarterback-hero crap. Act like a regular guy or god help me, I'll turn you right back to a mouse. You got me?"

Adamant rodent nodding ensues.

"What did you do to your wife?" Coffen asks Björn.

"I can't talk about it. I thought I was punishing her but all I did was make me hate myself."

Björn picks mousy Schumann up and puts the rodent in his jacket pocket. Then he lightly taps on the rodent-lump from outside the jacket a few times. The magician takes a deep breath, shuts his eyes, and there's a clap of thunder outside. Bob and Tilda look at each other. Björn takes another deep breath, and there's another clap of thunder. Finally he says, "Let evolution take its course." He taps the lump one last time.

And it's gone.

"Where is he?" Tilda asks.

That's when Schumann lopes in the front door of Taco Shed in his football uniform, standing full-sized, dressed as though Purdue might lock pigskinned-horns with Notre Dame any minute now.

"What happened?" he says, looking perplexed and disheveled.

"Where were you?" Tilda says.

"I don't know," he says. "I was suddenly standing out in the parking lot, and everything before it is hazy. I kind of remember feeling inconsequential, a sort of afterthought."

"Where are you coming from right now? Think hard," Coffen says. "Did you hear thunder just now?"

"I can't remember anything besides wearing a really warm fur coat," Schumann says.

"Holy shit," says Tilda.

"Boo-ya," Björn says.

"Are you being serious?" Coffen asks Schumann.

He nods and says, "Yeah, the fur coat is really all I can remember."

"What the almighty pigeon-toed fuck is going on?" Tilda screams.

Björn cracks up. "I keep telling you people I'm a sorcerer. But nobody wants to hear that. You all only want to rain hate down on my happy little shindig. Let me do my thing. Leave me and my well enough alone."

Bob wants to ask a flood of practical questions, feels the tug to disprove the possibility that Schumann had indeed been a mouse. The urge comes on strong, almost like a craving, a habit, but Coffen strangles it. The explanation isn't the point. Schumann's back. His wife has her husband. Little Schu, his dad. That's the point. That's all that matters, and Bob tries to embrace the mystery of it.

Schumann tells all that he's completely famished and asks if he can have a Mexican lasagna. Nobody objects, so he takes Coffen's straight out of his hands and digs in, signals that he's going to wait for everyone outside so he can try and think straight about this. Tilda altruistically volunteers to keep him company in the morning light—no doubt to test his memory of all she said to him while baby-sitting. He chomps away and Coffen watches her give him quite a speech. It makes Bob kind of sad, actually, thinking about Tilda pleading to her former mouse man, trying to make him want what she so badly wants.

"Good-bye," Björn says to Bob once the others are outside, finally removing his shades. His cheeks are dry. Moustache flattened on one half. "It's been interesting."

"You're not crying . . ."

"Not after the show last night. I'm done bending over backward for people. The world is full of ingrates."

"Magic is hard for us."

"Why?"

"I'm trying to turn over a new leaf and believe, but it's hard."

"Turn it over," says Björn. "Being a know-it-all is a terrible way to go through your life."

"I'm trying."

"What's the holdup?"

It's all so much for Coffen to take, to accept, to change years of his thinking. He never before has believed in magic, so why all of a sudden does he want to? And where's the valve on the parts of himself that don't want to believe? How can he turn them off, leaving only the open-minded parts of Bob? The ones that believe in Jane's chances to break the world record. Believe in Björn's dark arts prowess.

"Hello?" Björn says. "I asked what the holdup is."

"I'm probably the holdup."

"Do you want one more trick to prove I'm the real deal?"

"Yeah."

"Okay, this one will knock your socks off. This one will prove beyond any reasonable doubt that I am who I say I am."

"When's it going to happen?"

Björn laughs. "Stay tuned and keep your eyes open. I'm leaving this skid mark of sprawl one last spectacle. Do you like rainbows?"

"Rainbows?"

"Keep your eyes peeled," he says, then limps toward Taco Shed's door, putting on his sunglasses. He looks back at Bob and says, "I hope you turn over that leaf."

"Me, too."

Björn doesn't say anything to either Tilda or Schumann as he makes his way to his rental car. He speeds off.

Coffen makes his way outside, too.

"Can you drop me off at home?" Schumann says to Coffen.

"I'll drive you home, sweetie," Tilda offers.

"Thanks, but no. Bob and I need to talk about some stuff," he says.

"Don't we need to talk about some stuff as well?" Tilda asks. "We left a lot on the table last night."

"Yeah, but let me gather my thoughts, okay? I've been through quite an ordeal," says Schumann. His football uniform, which had always seemed symbolic and poetic and larger than life, now looks like any other costume—something a person puts on when he wants to see how the other half lives, when he wants to escape himself.

"Call me later?" she says, to which he nods, something timid in it, something defeated, victim of a fourth-quarter comeback that's come up short.

Tilda waves wildly as Coffen and Schumann start driving away from Taco Shed. The last thing Bob sees is Tilda bringing her hulky arms up, flexing like she's onstage in a bodybuilding competition. Bob's not the only person who's gotten out of his box this weekend; Tilda is taking a chance and opening up to her mouse man. Coffen smiles, looking back at Tilda's massive physique.

▪ The plight of the people of now ▪

Bob's nice enough to drive Schumann home when in actuality what he needs to do is hightail it to work for his team's Monday-morning status meeting, which will be getting underway in roughly half an hour. Coffen's boss is not a fan of late arrivals and often attempts to scold those of his underlings who traipse in after the clock has struck *late*, like a snobby professor sarcastically welcoming a tardy undergrad to class.

"Well, that was quite a weekend you had, Reasons with His Fists," Coffen says.

"Please don't call me that."

"What are you going to tell your wife?"

"As far as they're concerned, I've been on the couch watching the boob tube the whole time they were gone. And that's exactly what I will be doing from now on. My competitive streak has been cauterized. I thought I wanted to relive my glory days, but I don't. I'm not that person anymore."

Bob is appalled: "Jesus, you really are a mouse."

"What?"

"You don't think she deserves to know the truth?"

"I know the truth. That's what matters."

"I bet she'd disagree with that."

"The important thing is that I'm going to be a better man now."

"I bet she'd think the important thing is that you had sex with Tilda."

It disappoints Coffen that Schumann isn't going to level with his missus, but then Bob figures he has so much to worry about in his own life that he can't try to control how Schumann's going to handle things. At the very least, it sounds like Coffen will never endure another cameo from Reasons with His Fists. Thank Christ for pigskinned miracles.

Plus, and maybe this is the heart of the matter, Coffen sees Schumann for what he is: confused, sad, and broken, like so many others their age. Like Bob. Confused about their role in the world. A football game. A video game. It all adds up to the same thing. A way to escape how grueling reality can be, all the responsibilities, all the worries. There's good stuff, too, as Tilda says, between the cops, monsters, prudes, and mice, but you have to hunt for it, or the routine can pull you under.

"You're not going to tattle on me, are you?" Schumann asks.

"On one condition."

"What?"

"For one week, starting now, I want you to take a steady dose of Scout'sHonor!®"

"Why?"

"So you know when you lie," Coffen says. "I want you to be aware when you lie to your wife."

"What good will that do?"

"She won't know, but you will."

"I can't walk around all week bleeding from my nose, Bob."

"Exactly why Scout'sHonor!® works so well. Nobody can

afford to bleed all week long. Our lives are busy. Wonder what would happen if you don't lie to her but come clean about everything?"

"I don't want to come clean. And because you don't cheat on Jane, you're no perfect husband yourself. Don't you lie to her about other stuff?"

"I more leave stuff out than lie."

"Like what?"

"Like most of my real feelings."

"Isn't that lying?" Schumann says. "You should take Scout'sHonor!® too. Let the pill decide what's lying and what isn't."

He's spot-on. No disputing that. If one of Coffen's goals going forward is to do right by his people, then he has to find out all the facts. Try to be honest about everything, even issues he's previously avoided or downplayed or gone dumb about. Bob should go into his future with his eyes open as to when he's being dishonest. A week of Scout'sHonor!® will help keep him on track.

"Fine," Coffen says. "I'll do it."

"Right on. Good man. You take it for a week and after your time is up, maybe I'll decide to take it once we see how it works on you. That makes perfect sense."

"Take it or I tattle."

"What if I bleed to death?" Schumann whines.

"Stop being so selfish and you won't bleed to death."

"It's not that easy. You can't stop cold turkey."

"Choice is yours, Schumann. But I'll rat you out."

"These are the moments I know you never played on a football team. Teammates have each other's backs no matter what, until the game clock of life expires."

"What's it going to be?"

"What choice do I have? I'll take them and try not to bleed to death," Schumann says. "But if I do die, you can have my bagpipes. Every time you look at them remember that you murdered me with your truth pills."

"I can live with that."

They shake on it. He squeezes Bob's hand hard. Really hard. Hard enough that Coffen winces and emits a little girly yelp.

For the first time during the conversation, Schumann smiles, still crushing Coffen's hand. "Now who's peeping like a mouse," he says.

■ ■ ■

After dumping Schumann at home, Coffen makes it to the status meeting with ten minutes to spare. It's just him and Malcolm Dumper in the conference room, Coffen's young cohorts only arriving seconds before these meetings commence, risking late arrivals to maintain a persona of youthful ambivalence to structure, rules, the asinine consideration of other people's time.

Dumper is plopped on a beanbag, while Coffen hooks his laptop up to the overhead projector, so Scroo Dat Pooch will appear on the large white screen.

"Are you excited about your unveiling this morning, Coffen?"

"I'm excited to see what you think of it."

"I bet the Great One will love it like a bee loves smelling the roses."

"I hope you love these roses."

"We still need to have that dinner we've been talking about for years," Malcolm says.

"Yes, you'll have to come by the house sometime soon."

"Is your roof helipad-friendly?"

"I doubt it," says Coffen, "but I'm not sure."

"That means no. I won't make that mistake again. One mighty big check I had to write those buffoons who are too dumb to know the specifications of their own roof. While we're alone, I wanted to tell you that the layoffs I was mentioning are probably going to happen soon for some of our teammates. We need to whittle some pudge. And while we'll miss those members of our family who are no longer our teammates, truthfully, it probably could not come at a more ideal time for them to take a hiatus. They'll thank me in the long run. Go to Paris. Go backpacking. Fish in Alaska. Big things are afoot outside these walls."

"Big things are about to be afoot inside these walls, too," Coffen says. "Thanks for letting me know."

"I'm pro-information. I want my people knowing as much as my people can know. Especially those who are plock-worthy. Those who hold plocks hold a special place in my heart. Some things, of course, are for my eyes and ears only. Heavy is the head that wears the crown, if you get my drift. Don't worry about the pudge purge for now. Hopefully, your new game will help the layoffs be more of a simple cleansing than an all-out flush."

"I'm glad there's no pressure."

The team scampers into the conference room, planting themselves on various beanbags.

"We're all yours, Bob," Dumper says, smiling.

Coffen launches Scroo Dat Pooch. What makes this tricky is the possibility, nay, the probability that Dumper won't much care about the game's feel, the game's overall look. It's conceivable that he won't be concerned with such analytical components once he observes that Malcolm Dumper himself is the main character of the game, the head honcho of pooch screwing.

Bob has used a JPEG of Dumper's face to build the avatar, so the likeness is top-notch. It's almost a perfect match. And if Bob is too biased to make any objective observations about the facial likeness, as the test level launches, all of his teammates crack up and clap. Everybody in the conference room, except Dumper, is hysterical and nothing's even happened yet.

All that's on the screen is Dumper in his signature Gretzky sweater, #99.

All that's up there is Dumper and his big, thick tongue lolling stupidly from his mouth.

All that's there is Malcolm Dumper licking his filthy, bestiality-loving chops.

Kiss's "Rock and Roll All Nite" starts playing in the game.

All Bob's teammates tap their feet.

The mouth-breather says, "Awesome!"

Coffen is the only one standing in the conference room. His movements control the avatar. He now marches in place, his movements moving the Malcolm in the game. It's an empty cityscape. Malcolm prowling the barren street. Then, over behind some dented garbage cans, he spots a collie. It's looking generally frightened. Coffen's even incorporated some audio: a sad, furtive series of whimpers and whines coming from the collie.

Coffen runs in place, quickly moving Malcolm toward the crying dog. Malcolm leans down and pets the mutt, strokes its head. A voice comes from the game, Malcolm saying, "There, there. There, there. Shhh. Hey, do you like to party?"

The collie turns its head to look at whoever is playing the game. The dog's eyes bulge, seeming to say: *Did this creep just say what I think he said?*

Seconds later on the screen, Malcolm is undoing his belt and dropping his trousers.

Seconds later, he picks up the collie and mounts the poor thing.

Bob furiously pumps his hips in the conference room.

"Scroo dat pooch!" says the avatar of Malcolm, giving the hang-loose sign.

His teammates go crazy.

Coffen is practically hyperventilating.

The faster Bob pumps, a series of graphics appear above Malcolm's head—lightning bolts, throbbing hearts, pulsing stars. Bob goes as fast as his out-of-shape physique can handle and about twenty seconds later a message flashes across the center of the action:

Money shot!

Malcolm finishes giving his business to the dog.

Coffen gives his hips one last pump.

The mouth-breather whistles.

Once Malcolm's done sullying the collie, he sets the dog down and it wanders off with an awkward gait. Then the avatar pulls up his pants, buckles his belt. Then he says, "Me want the next one."

Bob says to his teammates and Malcolm, "That's all I had time to put together, but you can see the direction. From here, he'd move on to the next breed. What do you think?"

None of the teammates utter a peep. Everyone's waiting for Dumper to take point on this one. It's tough to read the boss's face, utterly blank of legible expression, tongue stowed away.

Coffen braces himself for the worst: security being called, roughing him up a bit on the walk from the building. Dumper refusing to honor his three-hundred-plus hours of paid time off. Dumper slandering his name with every contact he's ever made in the business, making it almost impossible for Bob to get another gig. It's a risk but one Coffen has to take; he sees no other way. He has to get fired. He needs permission to never come back here, as sick as that sounds. He won't do it on his own.

Finally, Dumper says, "I doubt I'm alone in wanting to heap congratulations on top of you like syrup on pancakes. I asked for edgy and you gave me edgy. It's extreme, but I think the targeted demo will froth for it."

"You like it?" Bob asks.

"It's exactly what I hoped for."

"Really? What about the avatar? Do you like his look?"

"What a dope! I love how he's dressed like your average Tom, Dick, or Harry. It's actually funnier that you didn't make him some creep. He looks like any working stiff." Dumper starts laughing. "A working stiff who likes to boink dogs."

"I'm surprised you like it," Bob says.

"You are a genius," Dumper says. "Isn't he a genius, gang?"

"Yes, yes," the teammates say, still howling. "He is indeed a genius!"

Coffen panics. Getting fired is the only way to get out of this job. He's not strong enough to do it on his own. He'll never make the change without being shoved, like a baby bird being heaved from the nest, a fledgling forced to fly under its own power.

Everything Bob once loved about building games is gone. It's been tarnished, denigrated. It's digressed from art to the ultimate farce, and it's his own fault. Nobody made him stay at DG. Nobody made him earn that fucking plock. He acted through his inaction. He chose a path by default. Scroo Dat Pooch and these kinds of imbecilic games are futile. He can get back to his art—he can build new ones, he will build new ones—games that are fun and smart at the same time. The two don't have to be mutually exclusive. Escapism doesn't require the inane. Yes, his next title will be about simply preserving your sense of self—or re-establishing a sense of self you've let rust. A sense of self that hasn't gotten the necessary attention. The game doesn't need an antagonist hopped up on mutated genetics. It doesn't need lasers. Or cannibals. It doesn't need Navy SEALs infected with a flesh-eating virus or vampires hunting you down or werewolves capturing you in a corner, licking their chops, eyeballing you as their next square meal. It doesn't need to take place on another planet. Doesn't need terrorists or dinosaurs or nuclear weapons or mutated crocodiles. Psychopaths aren't a necessary ingredient. Rogue pooch-screwers aren't foundational elements. No, the peril is right here. Peril covers more of the earth than the oceans. Peril is around us with every gasp, each lap around the sun, every whirl on the axis. Every sunup, sundown. Every eclipse. Every greenhouse gas. Every oil spill. Every endangered species. Every unfounded fear. Every founded fear. Every nightmare. Every diagnosis. Every time an alcoholic takes that next sip. Every gambler losing the mortgage money. Every affair. Every backhand. Every abandonment. Every deception. Every time a family falls apart. Every divorce. Every life. Each life. Bob's life. Your life. The peril is simple. The peril is us. It's the plight of the people of now.

"You guys got my green light," Dumper says. "Build this bad boy. Make it a masterpiece."

"You can keep the plock," says Bob. "Robert's days are done."

"You're taking a personal day?" Dumper asks.

"You've seen the last of Robert Coffen."

"What?"

"Robert's officially stepping down."

"What about the new game?"

"Have him do it," Coffen says and points at the mouth-breather.

"You're quitting?"

And that's that. There's no screaming scene. He doesn't demean Dumper with a melody of profanity. No need to go down in any kind of spectacle—he already tried that by building the damn game and it didn't work. Seems the only way for him to leave this place is of his own accord. Under his own power. And there's no time like the present. Might as well march out. So he struts from the conference room, past his teammates and the beanbags. Past Dumper and LapLand and its lifeguards. Past the whole preschool of his coworkers. He sees their young faces. He sees their futures. And while walking outside, he finally sees freedom.

▪ Geraldine the giant squid ▪

Coffen camouflages his spying. Hiding in plain sight. All afternoon and evening, he's another anonymous member of the health club relaxing by the outdoor pool, safety in numbers. He's another sucker kicking up his heels on a chaise lounge and soaking up some sunshine. Nobody pays him any mind, even though he has a pair of binoculars and spends most of his time aiming them through the huge window and toward the indoor pool, where Jane is trying to break the world's record for treading water.

Bob respects Jane's wishes, heard her loud and clear when she uninvited him to stand by the pool and purr moral support. Nobody, not even Gotthorm, knows more than Bob about how much Jane wants to accomplish this remarkable feat, and so he follows her instructions, stations himself outside the confines of the building, hunkering down for some average, run-of-the-mill peeping. She's none the wiser to his presence and Coffen can feel as if he's offering every nickel of his support, safely stationed away from her.

Unless Bob's binoculars deceive him, Jane is doing great thus far. She's been in the water for about five hours. She looks relaxed. Braids hidden under a swim cap.

Erma is there with Brent and Margot. The kids sit in

folding chairs and fiddle with their favorite devices: Brent, his phone; Margot, her iPad.

There's also a judge present: the stickler who oversees if in fact Jane's able to tread water eighty-six hours straight. It's a woman, probably in her forties. She holds a clipboard, which strikes Bob as odd. What can there possibly be to take notes about? Either Jane breaks the record or she doesn't, but the judge periodically scribbles something mysterious down.

And of course, Gotthorm, clad in his red Speedo. He's right next to the pool, the closest one to her. He has some kind of huge taxidermied fish and he glides it around in his arms; some kind of visual aid, Coffen assumes. Bob wishes he could read lips, wonders what Gotthorm and the bulge whisper to his wife while the fish dances in his arms.

The problem comes when a voice pipes over the intercom system and says, "We will be closing in ten minutes. All members need to leave the club in ten minutes, please."

Bob is relatively prepared for this. He has a plan, of sorts. There's a thought to how he can evade detection. Of sorts. Coffen's not the most stealth fella, but he thinks he can hide behind the hut that houses the pool's cleaning supplies. Once it seems like most of the lights are off in the facility, he'll come back out and spy more.

He has a ski jacket. He has a blanket. He has a thermos of coffee and fifteen Mexican lasagnas.

He has everything he needs to support his wife from one hundred feet away.

That first night is lonely. About 10:30 PM, Erma and the kids leave. Bob's sure they'll be back some time in the morning, but he doesn't like the idea that it's only Gotthorm and the judge with Jane. She should have a bigger cheering section. She should have French Kiss playing songs to keep her alert. He almost calls Ace before realizing that's a terrible idea. His only job is to stay out of sight, and he's not going to screw it up.

But apparently he's already screwed it up. It's not half an hour later and Gotthorm comes out to where he's hiding, sort of wedged under a chaise lounge.

"What's that?" Bob asks, pointing at the big taxidermied fish in Gotthorm's hands.

"It's an African pompano."

"But why do you have it?"

"A mermaid has the upper body of a human and the tail of a fish."

"Thanks for refreshing my memory."

"Jane needs to be supported by both her land family and those family members from under the sea."

"And that stuffed fish is like an aquatic cousin?"

"I'm going to let you stay and watch us from out here," Gotthorm says. "But you can't come inside and Jane won't know you're present."

"Why can't I come in and cheer her on?"

"No one cheers on a piece of sea grass, being bandied by the tide."

"Right, but she's . . ."

"Nobody applauds a jellyfish feeding on plankton."

"That's my human wife in there."

"Jane is transcending human endurance. She is of two worlds right now. And her mind needs to be like this fish's mind." He moves the taxidermied thing in an arcing motion. "You pollute her state of nothingness."

Gotthorm turns and starts walking back toward the indoor pool, leaving Bob and his binoculars all by their lonesome.

■ ■ ■

About 4:00 AM something sort of beautiful happens. Gotthorm gets into the pool with a bottle of Gatorade and an energy bar. He approaches Jane. Slowly, she seems to emerge from her trance, her nothingness, and she slowly drinks the whole Gatorade, eats the snack. Then she shuts her eyes again and returns to her puckered breathing.

Coffen climbs into the empty lifeguard chair, the perch giving him a better view. He watches Jane in awe. Watches and feels washed with affection.

■ ■ ■

Tuesday looks a lot like Monday. Besides intermittent trips into the locker room to relieve himself, Coffen stays fixed to the outdoor pool deck, spying with grave intensity, snacking on his stash of Mexican lasagnas.

If Coffen's calculations are correct, she's been treading water for twenty-nine hours now.

And while he can't see her legs working in the pool, he can see her face, her arms, her cohesive motions. Gotthorm is right—there is something otherworldly in the way her body moves.

Erma, Margot, and Brent are back.

Apparently, the judges rotate to stay alert. The woman who was there the day before is now gone. A small gentleman is positioned close to the pool, scrutinizing each of Jane's strokes, clutching a clipboard of his very own.

Bob texts his kids the same message: *How's our girl doing?*

Margot: *fine*

Brent: *you mean mom?*

Bob: *Think good thoughts for her!*

Neither of them knows he's out there, hiding with the masses on the congested pool deck. He figures it's better to keep them in the dark about his distant attendance, so they don't accidentally tell Erma, who would probably call the cops on him. Or worse, buy a stun gun and handle things herself.

■ ■ ■

Gotthorm comes out again to chat with Coffen late Tuesday, around 11:00 PM. The health club is closed. He's not carrying the African pompano this time, but instead is eating a banana.

"Aren't you cold?" Bob says, pointing at his Speedo.

"I'm Nordic."

"Don't remind me. How's she doing?"

"She is accepting the ocean as another home. And it is accepting her."

Bob fights back laughter. Why is it that the first thing through Coffen's stupid mind is a wisecrack? Here his wife is going on forty hours straight of treading water and all he wants to do is say something snide to Gotthorm: How is a heated indoor pool anything like the open ocean?

He stops himself, embarrassed. Why can't he focus on

what's important? He catches himself, composes himself, then says to Gotthorm, "She's going to do it this time."

The coach snorts. "Too soon to know. She's made it this far before."

"This time's different. I can tell."

"Fish swim forever," Gotthorm says.

■ ■ ■

Wednesday looks a lot like Tuesday. It's a bit after high noon. Coffen has run into the locker room to shower, shit, and brush his teeth, and then flees back to the pool deck to eat another Mexican lasagna—a snack that doesn't age well. Each bite a chore. Each bite probable food poisoning.

Jane's just crossed the fifty-hour plateau, which puts her nine hours away from her personal best. Nine hours away from uncharted waters.

■ ■ ■

That night, Gotthorm doesn't come out to talk to Bob, which he takes as a bad sign. Coffen's up on the lifeguard chair, peering in at them. The coach looks worried, leaning down and talking a lot to Jane as she treads. The African pompano has been thrust to the side. This can't be good.

Erma, Margot, and Brent have gone home to get some sleep. The same judge is there, alert as always, clipboard in his hands.

Coffen channels his inner Gotthorm, thinking to himself, *Why would a fish need any words of encouragement to keep on swimming?*

Through the binoculars, Jane appears no different. Her

eyes are closed. She paddles and sways her limbs with the same nimble fluidity. She breathes her puckered breaths.

But Gotthorm's shift in demeanor has Bob flustered, and a flustered Bob Coffen isn't known for shrewd decision-making. Pretty soon, he's creeping up toward the window. Pretty soon, he's pantomiming a big thumbs-up with a simultaneous shrug of the shoulders to Gotthorm, who responds only with pursed lips and a shaking head.

■ ■ ■

At 5:00 AM on Thursday, Jane's been treading for sixty-seven hours, and this is the moment when her eyes pop open. The skin tone changes, going pale. Her rhythmic, puckering breaths go into shallower, almost panic-stricken sucks of air. Her head slips a bit under the water. She catches herself, rights her stroke, but it's the first slip she's made.

Coffen sees all this through the window. Face pressed right up to the glass.

Coffen sees this and wants so badly to whisper in her ear: *You've come this far. You can do it. You can do anything in the world you put your mind to.*

■ ■ ■

Gotthorm comes out to the crowded pool deck at 10:00 AM. He has the exhausted look of a surgeon who's been doing his best to keep a patient alive, but whose tireless efforts might be in vain.

"Have you gotten any sleep?" Bob asks.

"We're at seventy-two hours."

"She's really struggling, it looks like."

"She's exhausted."

"Will she make it?"

"I worry she'll cramp soon."

"And that's it?"

"Fish swim until they die," says Gotthorm.

"Before you said that fish swim forever."

"Nobody can wiggle a mackerel's tail but that very fish."

"Is there any way to help her?"

"You are in your own competition, like Jane and me," Gotthorm says. "You've been here as many hours as us. You've been competing. I'm impressed. You are stronger than you look."

"Is that a compliment?"

"She needs more strength. She's used up all her dedication to me, used up all her personal willpower. She's drawn all the fuel she can from having your children present. Now it's up to Jane to keep her humanness shut off. She has to stay aquatic or she'll give in to fatigue."

"Maybe her fish-ness has gotten her this far, but she needs her humanness to cross the finish line," says Bob.

"That doesn't make any sense," Gotthorm says. "Only the ocean can baptize her. Those of us trapped on land, we are powerless to help."

It's certainly not the intention of Gotthorm to plant any seeds in the head of a certain Bob Coffen. That's the last thing the coach is trying to do. What is he trying to do anyway? Why does he keep coming outside acting chummy with Bob? All Coffen can figure is that he's impressed Gotthorm with this round-the-clock peeping and has miraculously weaseled into his good graces.

The seed that has been planted in Bob now drills down

into his cranium and an idea grows. Time lapse. The seed is buried and the sprout shoves up out of the soil in one fell swoop. The seed itself is in these previous words from Gotthorm: "Those of us trapped on land, we are powerless to help." And the idea growing inside Bob's head is this: If the coach's fish philosophy seems as if it's failing, really failing—Jane's head going underwater, Jane seeming as if she's going to come up short of the world record—if this happens, then Bob Coffen has a plan to help her with some good old-fashioned humanness.

"I need to get back to her," Gotthorm says, starting his Speedoed strut back toward the indoor pool. "The sea can flick a catamaran like it's a cigarette butt. The ocean can hack up a submarine like a wad of gristle from a fat man's throat after the Heimlich maneuver."

"I still say she has some human in there," says Bob.

"I pray not," Gotthorm says.

■ ■ ■

The club closes at 7:00 PM, which happens to be the eighty-one hour mark. At midnight—when the plock strikes its only time—she'll have broken the record.

Once the outside deck clears of other club members, Coffen climbs back up on the lifeguard perch to get the best view. Jane's once lovely rhythm is shot. Her puckered breathing seems more like someone waking from a nightmare. Stunned. Scared. She is pale. Her eyes are wide open, blinking lots.

Erma, Margot, and Brent are no longer there. Gotthorm sits on the side of the pool and says things to Jane—words Bob so badly wants to hear. He so badly wants to help. On one hand, sure, he wants to respect her wishes to stay away, yet also he wants to disassemble those wishes. Obviously, they're not the right ones. He hasn't been near the pool and it's clear to anybody's eyeballs that she's about to go under. She's about to lose. And Bob Coffen isn't about to let that happen, not without a fight, not without trying to help her.

Jane is not an urchin.

Jane is no manatee.

She's not an anemone or a dolphin or a cuttlefish.

Jane's no shark.

She is a human, a woman, his wife. This is real life, and she needs to hear real encouragement, needs to know her family believes in her. Whether Jane knows it or not, she needs her husband to be there.

Coffen throws the binoculars down, hops off the life-guard chair. He runs toward the door to the men's locker room. It's locked. Of course. They've shut down for the evening. He knocks on it. Nobody answers. Duh. He slams his shoulder into it. Twice. Four times. Six.

Why is breaking down doors so easy on television? That's going to bruise.

He kicks it. He moves and tries the door to the women's locker room, too. No luck. No shoulder slams. No kicks. Think. Coffen has little time. She looked so pale. No choice but to try and lure Gotthorm to invite Bob inside. So he runs to the huge window. So he knocks on it. So he waves at Gotthorm. The judge looks over. Gotthorm only shakes his head. Gotthorm only keeps talking to Jane. Coffen only keeps knocking. What can he do? What options are there? He's trying to bring Jane her humanness. He has to help her. Jane pulls her swim cap off. It drifts in the water like a small octopus. Reminds Coffen of their first date. Their first online date. In the chat room. In the Italian restaurant. Jane said a two-ton squid escaped the zoo. It lived under her bed. She fed it a steady diet of saltwater taffy. Bob fell in love with her right then. Wanted to kiss her imagination right on the mouth. Imaginations should have mouths. Imaginations should have great big puckering lips. Imaginations should sit on people's shoulders like mousy Schumann had been sitting on Bob's. Coffen needs to get inside. Needs to tell Jane she's not a fish. Needs to tell Jane that she's a gorgeous woman. He should mention he quit his job. But not until later. Not until she's broken the record. After that the job thing won't be so bad, maybe. The doors are locked. He's knocking on the window and Gotthorm and the judge don't move to let him in. Her swim cap starts to sink. Bob can't see Jane's face and he knocks harder. She said that every squid who ever escaped the zoo after that first one always came to her house. Word travels fast with squid. Everybody knows that. Nobody's going to help Bob get in there. This is going to be a Bob-only enterprise if entering the indoor poolroom is his chief pursuit. Coffen runs back to the outdoor deck. Coffen is getting good at throwing things. Ask that flowerpot. He is no longer afraid of consequences born from the sound of shattering.

Coffen says, "Bob is me."

He doesn't throw the chaise lounge at the window so much as he uses it as a kind of battering ram and it works. The window explodes. The judge's face is sort of scared. He clutches the clipboard to his chest like it's a crying baby. Gotthorm's face is not scared so much but wearing a wondrous *What the hell?* Bob can no longer see the sinking swim cap. Bob climbs through the busted window. Bob is still fully clothed. Bob is still wearing shoes. There are problems with his plan. He is saying to the judge, "Will she be disqualified if I enter the water but I don't touch her or interfere in any way?" and the judge is saying, "Who are you?" and Gotthorm is saying, "That is her husband," and the judge is saying, "What's wrong with using the door?" and Gotthorm is saying, "What are you doing?" and Coffen is saying to the judge, "Can I get in the pool so long as I don't physically aid her?" and the judge nods, *Sure, do it, go ahead, you window-shatterer.*

So:

Fully clothed Bob Coffen leaps into the water. About twenty feet away from his wife. Jane is really struggling. Bob swims over, not getting too close. Judges probably love to issue disqualifications and Coffen won't give the smug prick the satisfaction. Her swim cap is flat on the bottom of the pool. Bob is treading water maybe ten feet away from her now.

He says, "Jane, it's me, Bob. You're almost there. You almost have the record. You can do it. I know you can do it. Don't give up now."

Jane doesn't say anything. She keeps her head above the surface. But barely. Her strokes are arrhythmic, all over the place.

Bob says, "You're only about four hours away from the record."

The judge says, "Five hours, eleven minutes."

Bob says, "You're only five hours and eleven minutes away from the record."

Jane doesn't say a word.

Bob says, "Do you remember a two-ton squid that escaped from the zoo? You told me that it snuck in your bedroom window and hid under your bed. You fed it salt-water taffy."

"I named it," Jane says, eyes finally focusing on Bob.

"What did you name it?"

"Geraldine."

"How did you know it was a girl?"

"She chewed her taffy in a very feminine way."

"Geraldine the giant squid," says Bob.

"What are you doing here?" Jane asks.

"Gotthorm invited me. He said that all your training has worked perfectly—that you're the best athlete he's ever trained. But he thought you might be getting tired and he asked if I wanted to tread water with you for the last five hours."

The judge says, "Five hours, nine minutes."

Bob says, "Five hours and nine minutes."

Jane says, "You're going to tread water for five hours and nine minutes?"

Bob says, "Only if you'll do it with me."

Gotthorm smiles at Coffen: "Yeah, Jane, we thought that seeing your husband might help you finish it off."

"Yes, we did," Bob says, already wishing he'd taken off his shoes.

"Are the kids here, too?" Jane says.

"I can call your mom," Gotthorm says. "She can bring them back. They were going to set an alarm and return at midnight if you broke the record. Would you like them back here now?"

"Yes," Jane says.

Gotthorm goes to call Erma.

The judge stands on the side.

Bob bobs. Jane bobs.

Jane says, "I'm so fucking tired."

Bob says, "A porpoise is one with the water."

Jane says, "Don't make me laugh right now."

Bob says, "Sea otters look like my uncle Mickey."

Jane says, "What are you doing in here with me?"

Bob says, "I needed some exercise."

Jane says, "I don't think we can do this."

Bob says, "Watch us."

Five hours and nine minutes is what Jane needs. What Bob needs, too. He has a sturdy guilt about doubting her likelihood of breaking the record earlier and the only way to purge it is this.

Getting rid of his guilt is like sucking venom from a wound: Coffen has to draw his doubt out of his system or it will poison him, poison them, and he's not going to let that happen. If she can make it well over eighty hours in the pool, Bob can handle five hours and change.

Bob tries visualization to fight his fatigue: he and Jane are in a bathtub, relaxing. It's not working. He tries counting his exhalations, inhalations, tries humming a tune to himself. Nothing seems to ease his exhaustion. He tries silently chanting, *We need five hours and nine minutes in total, five hours and nine minutes, five hours and nine minutes . . .*

"How much time has gone by?" says Bob after half an hour.

"*Nei, nei,*" Gotthorm says. "Kelp can't decipher the clock."

Bob looks at Jane. She seems to have stabilized, her stroke improving. She's not as pale as before. Her breathing's steady. Her eyes are shut.

Coffen copies her, shuts his eyes, too. Trying to rally. He has no idea that you can sweat so much while swimming.

Has no idea how woozy an individual can get simply treading water. Certainly, he has no idea that you can almost hyperventilate just staying in the same place, flailing your arms and legs, head slipping under the water every now and again.

The fatigue and cramping pain poking up his thighs are getting worse.

He notices he's hungry.

Notices his vision isn't quite double, per se, but it's certainly more than single.

And yet there's something about Bob Coffen that's enjoying this arduous task. Digs the exertion and mounting headache. Thrives on how thirsty he is.

He accidentally swallows the chlorinated water and coughs. The taste left in his mouth is salty, almost like a cured meat.

We need five hours and nine minutes, keeps ringing in Bob's mind.

▪ Strip, jump ▪

"Dad, are you okay?" Margot says.

"What happened?"

"You almost drowned."

"What?"

"He had to pull you out."

"Who?"

"Gotthorm."

"Huh?"

"He gave you mouth-to-mouth."

"Oh, no."

"You were dead, I think, for a minute or so," she says.

"Did you watch Gotthorm give me mouth-to-mouth?"

"Yes."

"Brent, too?"

"Uh-huh."

"Jesus, kill me."

"G-Ma watched with us."

"Of course she did."

"Mom couldn't watch because she was finishing up."

"Where's your mom?"

"Talking to those reporters. I filmed it for you."

"She really made it?" Bob sits up on the pool deck, still

in his soaked clothes, and peers over at Jane talking with two reporters.

"Yeah. She finished."

Gotthorm walks over to Coffen and Margot. "You needed to tread water for five hours and eleven minutes," he says. "You made it about five hours and two minutes."

"Thanks for saving my life."

"I had no choice; your kids were here."

"Thanks anyway."

"You made it much longer than I thought you would. You have fight in you."

"I tried."

"You succeeded," Gotthorm says. "She did it. That's what you were trying to do."

"I guess."

"There was some human still inside her. You were right, Bob. Do you want me to call an ambulance? You seem fine to me. I've almost drowned about fifty times playing water polo over the years."

"I guess I'm fine."

"You're more than fine. She wouldn't have broken it without your help," Gotthorm says.

"Yeah, good job, Dad," says Margot. "Can I film you?"

"Doing what?"

"Basking in your glory," she says.

Bob nods and says, "Go ahead."

"Ro's going to flip when she sees all this footage. Okay, action!"

Coffen smiles as his daughter shoots him sitting there. He'll never say it to her because it would ruin everything, but he can tell: She's proud of him. No doubt about it.

"Do you have any words for your fans?" Margot asks, beaming.

"Treading water is harder than it looks."

■ ■ ■

The two reporters—one columnist, one photographer—take pictures, nab their quotes. Both Jane and Gotthorm are interviewed. Bob sits with his mother-in-law, daughter, and son on some metal bleachers, waiting for Jane to finish up the festivities.

"I'm glad you're okay," Brent says.

"Me too."

"Next time, I want to go swimming."

"Go swimming right now if you want," Coffen says.

"I don't have my suit."

"Are you wearing underwear?"

The boy nods.

"Strip down and go in those. We need to get my shoes off the pool floor anyway. I took them off when I was treading. And your mom's swim cap is down there, as well. Do you want to go in, too, Margot?"

"Not a chance," she says.

"Can I really?" Brent asks.

"Strip, jump," Bob says.

The boy does just that, losing his clothes and leaping in, feet first. He swims down and gets Jane's cap, then Bob's shoes. He sets them on the side of the pool and gets to playing, swimming in little circles, holding his breath and diving down.

By the time Brent climbs out, Jane and Gotthorm are

done chatting with the press. They slowly walk over to the Coffens.

"I feel like I've been hit by a shovel," Jane says. "I want to eat a pizza and sleep for the rest of the week."

"Let's order a pizza," Brent says.

"You've earned it," Erma says to Jane. "A world champion in our family. Who would have thought that could ever happen? We're not a bad clan, but there's never been anything special about us."

"Now you have a daughter who lives on both land and sea," Gotthorm says.

"What's he talking about?" asks Erma.

"Never mind," Bob says. "Gotthorm, it's been interesting. You should come over to the house sometime. Do me a favor and wear pants."

"What about a wet suit?"

"Anything with more surface area."

"Are we really getting pizza so late at night?" Brent says.

"No restaurants are open," Jane says.

"We'll raid the frozen food section of the store," Bob says.

"I like those mozzarella melts," Margot says.

"Jalapeño poppers," Brent says.

"Fish sticks with extra tartar sauce," says Gotthorm.

"Let's buy everything we can," Jane says.

"We can stay up and watch movies," Brent says.

"I could eat some serious frozen pizza," Bob says.

"Are we finally ready to go home?" Jane asks.

They are. They do.

▪ The night rainbow ▪

Six days later and Bob Coffen can't believe his eyes. Björn has lived up to his promise to dazzle their suburb with a rainbow. Normally, Bob would try to dismiss this as a coincidence—it's just a rainbow, after all. He'd typically liken it to a hack palm reader saying vague things to desperate customers, allowing them to plug the info into their own lives. *You say the letter M is important in my future? I have a close friend who moved to Massachusetts last year and I miss her terribly.*

But this isn't your run-of-the-mill rainbow.

This is beyond any rational explanation.

First off, it's snowing cats and dogs outside and never in the history of this parochial town has a single flake fluttered from the atmosphere.

Second alarming, inexplicable fact is that the rainbow is happening at nighttime. It's been in the sky for the last half hour. Coffen's no kind of weather shaman, but he is a decently educated person, which means he knows that rainbows need the sun to shine light through moisture in the sky, triggering some kind of crazy refracting business between the raindrops and the light. This all somehow creates an arc of colors, a daytime sky hosting a rainbow. One at night in a snowstorm, however, is impossible.

A meteorologist might call the conditions *cataclysmic*.

The snow and night rainbow has prompted panic in the average citizen. The power is out, which means no cable TV, no Wi-Fi. Bob has retrieved their earthquake kit and is glued to the archaic AM radio to see what people are saying about the unexpected storm. Jane attempts to distract the kids with a project. Luckily, their oven is gas and so they prepare to bake chocolate chip cookies. Unluckily, the task is not sidetracking the kids: Margot is climbing the walls, trying to get a wireless signal on her iPad. Brent had been playing a video game on his phone, but the batteries died about ten minutes ago, no way to charge it, and the boy looks confused, a bit scared.

There's a startling, petrified chatter on the talk shows as Coffen cruises the band, the populous fearing the worst:

"Is it time to use the word 'Apocalypse'?" a man asks a disc jockey. "Can we safely assume that this is Judgment Day?"

The DJ stays on the bright side: "Why should we assume the worst? So it's never snowed like this in the history of our beautiful suburb, so what? Maybe this is simply an unexpected respite from our normal weather patterns. I'm not ready to preach doomsday. It's too early for that. Our next caller is Dwight. Welcome, sir. What do you think of our weather: angry god or anomaly?"

Bob thinks, *Please say anomaly, Dwight.*

Jane says to the kids, "Don't eat all the dough. We have to bake some."

Dwight sounds all mild manners and green tea and multivitamins at first, starting off with, "A couple inches of snow, fine, I can chock that up to a blip." Then he gets a bit more mania in his voice, "But we're talking two and a half feet over a few hours?" And finally full-throttle naked obscene chaos rumbles up his guts and throat and rockets out with space shuttles from his mouth, "This is insane! The beginning of the end! My advice to all is buy canned goods and water! Lots of canned goods! Hole up with loved ones and hoard your canned goods! If this keeps up, canned goods will be worth $100 a pop! Listen up, people, *canned goods!* Buy every canned good you can get your hands on!"

"Thanks, Dwight," says the disc jockey, "for that public service announcement. You heard it here first, people. Canned goods will be the new currency. Up next is Judy. Hi, Judy."

"Do you know what I've been doing since the snow started?"

"Do tell us."

"I've taken my binoculars out on my patio and have been searching the sky. My eyes have been combing the horizon, which ain't easy with the poor visibility from the snow, but I'm doing my best. Guess what I'm looking for?"

"Why, I'm sure I don't know, Judy, but I'll venture a guess to play along. Is the answer terrorists?"

"Fat chance, my friend," Judy says. "I'm out scouring the sky for flying pigs."

"Pigs can't fly," Brent says.

"It can't snow at sea level at this longitude and latitude, and that's happening," Margot says.

"Maybe it's time to turn that off," Jane says to Bob, molding the cookie dough into dime-sized balls, then placing them on a baking sheet.

"One sec," says Coffen.

"Brigades of flying pigs!" Judy says. "Squadrons of them.

Because believe it or not, that's the only thing that will make any sense of this. An innocent snowstorm? No way. It's never happened before. But if I see pigs fly into our town, then I'll know that this is the end of days and anything is possible. Sit back and wait for the invasion of the flying pigs."

"You heard it here first, folks. Judy's got her eyes peeled for pigs. And let's hope she doesn't see any. I don't know about you, but I'm not quite ready for the end of days. My queue is stuffed with classics and I still haven't climbed Everest. We need to take a quick break so enjoy these messages from our lovely sponsors . . ."

"Turn it off, Bob," Jane says. "We need you right now."

He clicks the radio off and walks into the kitchen. Coffen says to them, "The cookies smell great."

They're all waiting for the first batch to be done.

"Is it dangerous?" Brent says.

"The snow?" Bob asks.

"Maybe," Margot says.

"Of course it's not dangerous," Bob says.

"It's just like rain, sweetie," Jane says, "except it's frozen."

"Can we play in it?" Brent asks.

Bob and Jane look at each other, shrug.

Once the cookies are finished and they've each eaten one, they take the snowy bull by the horns, bundling themselves up and trekking out into the storm. Outside, it surprises Coffen how empty the streets are. He figured at least the subdivision children would be out building snowmen, having fights with mounds of pressed powder, something. Must be the mania of their parents keeping them cooped up inside, forced to stare out windows and wishing for a chance to play in it.

The four of them stand in the driveway, staring up at the night rainbow. It's showing all the colors of the spectrum, even purple. It's extra vivid because of the sky's blackness. The clouds around it light the rainbow with a hazy shimmer.

"It looks like it touches the ground over there," Brent says, pointing in the direction of the small park in the center of the subdivision's Y-shape. "Can we go look?"

"I don't see why not," Coffen says. "Jane?"

"Sure," she says.

"This is impossible," Margot says. "Rainbows aren't real at night."

"Maybe there's a pot of gold at the rainbow's end," says Brent.

"It's an optical illusion," his sister says. "It doesn't touch down over there. The rainbow is based on where you're standing. There's no such thing as the end of the rainbow."

"Maybe this one does touch down," Jane says to her. "According to you, there can't even be a rainbow at night."

Margot sighs and says, "This is stupid."

Coffen says to Brent, "If there is a pot of gold at the rainbow's end, we'll split any loot with you."

"Can I stay home? It's freezing," says Margot.

Bob talks in a terrible pirate accent: "You don't get a cut of the treasure unless you come along for the adventure."

She doesn't laugh. But she does sigh and come along. So there's that . . .

"Maybe you won't need a new job," Jane says, "if we strike it rich tonight."

"Try to talk the kids out of college," Bob says. "Then we can squeak by. Plus, now that Ace is teaching me to play the bass, I might become a rock star."

"That sounds really probable," she says and smiles at him.

And so the four of them push on into the snowy, rainbowed night. Tough trudging through the powder with their wonky, sinking steps. They walk to the end of the cul-de-sac. Coffen takes in the cars—how they're hidden under a blanket of snow. He remembers calling himself a fluorescent orange monster, covered in so much of the artificial stuff, hidden under all his failures. He rubs his hand across a car's bumper, knocking the snow off, inspecting what's underneath. Then he turns his gaze skyward, looking at all the flakes coming down, all of them white, not one orange flake targeting him.

They get to the park eventually. Smack in the middle of the snowy field is the rainbow's end. It comes down and kisses the snow.

Bob wonders how the HOA will handle this: Who shall be the recipient of a belligerent, bullying email about an unauthorized rainbow?

The Coffens are the only people out; they've got the place to themselves.

As they stand gawking at the thing, there's a lovely barrage of adjectives, one from each member of the family:

"Unbelievable!"

"Stupefying!"

"Cool!"

"Impossible!"

Then Coffen says, "I want to touch it."

He starts walking toward it.

His family follows.

They all reach the rainbow's end. It's about two feet wide, shaped cylindrically, and Bob puts his hand into the rainbow. For some reason, he'd expected the colors to be hot, like steam releasing from a teakettle, but it's no different temperature than the cold, snowy air. He moves his hand around in the light, watching it shift from red to orange to yellow, then green, blue, purple.

"Can I do it too?" Brent says.

"We all can," Coffen says.

And they all do, hands sticking in the colors. They are all deep in the night rainbow. Everyone's laughing! Margot moves her hand around in a motion like dribbling a basketball.

"Isn't this better than pretending to be at the Great Barrier Reef?" Coffen asks her, gloating that she's seeing something in the real world that she'll never see online.

But she doesn't answer, watches her colored hand continue to bounce the invisible ball, mesmerized.

"There's no treasure," says Brent.

"Yeah, there is," Coffen says.

"Why is the magic rainbow here?" Brent asks.

"That's a great question," Jane says.

"Probably Armageddon," Margot says.

"What's that?" Brent asks.

"It's nothing," Coffen says.

"I hope it never leaves," Brent says.

"That would be insane," Margot throws in, still bouncing her invisible basketball.

She's not far off. It would indeed be insane if the night rainbow rooted in this spot like some kind of monument. Coffen pauses at this idea: What would it be immortalizing? The plock marks the passing of ten years. What kind of shrine might the night rainbow be, inexplicably landing in their lives without reason or recourse or context or perspective? What's the big idea behind such wondrous alchemy?

In the end, who really cares?

Point is it's here.

Point is it's here and so are all the Coffens.

They stand together, their hands flexing and stretching colorfully in the night rainbow's rounded light. Bob's free hand has crept up over his heart again, like it had that first evening on Schumann's lawn. What's that ditty he's now humming? "Hail Purdue"?

No, actually Coffen happens to be performing his family's fight song: "Rock and Roll All Nite."

Jane smiles at his selection and says, "Would you have ever guessed something like this could happen to us?"

Bob Coffen looks at all the vibrant, rainbowed hands of his family. "Just lucky, I guess," he says, then picks up the tune where he left off.

Acknowledgments

I wouldn't have a career if it weren't for the tireless enthusiasm of independent booksellers. The work you do often goes unnoticed, so I want to thank you all from the bottom of my heart! We should all try and buy a book from an indie shop this week. Come on: you can do it.

Special thanks to Cooper Edens, author of *If You're Afraid of the Dark, Remember the Night Rainbow*. It's my favorite children's book, and I wanted to pay homage to it in *Fight Song*.

I'd also like to thank a couple of Dans: my editor, Dan Smetanka, who has a shrewd eye and a wise spirit: scribbling this book together was a blast. And to my agent, Dan Kirschen of ICM: I know I'm in good hands with you and am stoked to grow a career together.

Eric Obenauf read this book in manuscript form and gave me kickass feedback. Thanks for your continued support, old friend.

On an unrelated note, Bucky Sinister wrote a poem for my wedding, which has nothing to do with what we're talking about, except I want to say thanks to him one last time.

Thanks to my colleagues in the MFA program at the University of San Francisco, and also at Stanford's Online Writer's Studio.

I'm blessed to be surrounded by cerebral, strong, and beautiful women: Diane, Sarah, Margaret, Jessica, Katy, Shana, Rochelle, Chellis, Aubrey, Veronica.

My wife, Leota Antoinette, is my perfect playmate. We have so much fun together it should be illegal, but I'm sure thankful it isn't.

About the Author

Joshua Mohr is the author of the novels *Termite Parade* (a *New York Times Book Review* Editor's Choice selection), *Some Things that Meant the World to Me* (one of *O Magazine*'s Top 10 reads of 2009 and a *San Francisco Chronicle* bestseller), and *Damascus*, published in the fall of 2011 to much critical acclaim. Mohr teaches in the MFA program at the University of San Francisco.